THE TIES THAT BIND

5 ORIGINAL SMALL TOWN RELATIONSHIP SHORT STORIES THAT INSPIRE

J. A. BOUMA

EmmausWay
P R E S S

INTRODUCTION

Last year, I'd been kicking around the idea of creating a fictional smallish town in West Michigan for several months, thinking it could be a fun way to tell the stories of people living life while exploring faith, taking a page out of Stephen King's playbook with Castle Rock, Maine, and John Grisham's Clanton, Mississippi.

Then the Great Pandemic of 2020 hit, and it seemed like the perfect time to kick off the project! After all, I was stuck inside like most people with lots of time on my hands. Figured I should keep busy, because as they say: idle hands are the devil's tools! Sounded like great fun anyway, spending my newfound time with a new set of characters in a new world outside my normal world that had been blown up by a crazy virus, but also something different from the usual story world of my existing fiction.

Thus was born Mill Creek Junction, as well as a host of characters who show up in the Christmas-themed collection of original short stories set in the small Midwest town.

And if there is anything that is true about small towns, it's that relationships are the ties that bind the community together. Any community, really, small town or not. But from my experience and own childhood in a small Midwest town, they're the glue of life.

So, here's to relationships, of all sorts. And here's a collection of five original short stories that tell of those relationships.

From a chance-encounter meet-cute between two people from opposite sides of the tracks on New Years Eve leading to a connection that leads to something more. To a night on the countryside between friends that leads to a rollicking adventure only conjured by small-town living.

Then there's the small-town law firm of three partners struggling to make ends meet, and a revelation about what matters most. The baton-passing between one pastor and another, one generation to another, and all the thoughts and feelings about that. Ending with a group of friends celebrating a holiday that reminds them they've got all they need: each other.

Relationships are the stuff of life, especially small-town living. Which makes sense, as the Book of Ecclesiastes points out in chapter 4:

Two are better than one, because they have a good reward for their toil. For if they fall, one will lift up the other; but woe to one who is alone and falls and does not have another to help. Again, if two lie together, they keep warm; but how can one keep warm alone? And though one might prevail against another, two will withstand one. A threefold cord is not quickly broken.

Wise words for an age forgetting what matters most. You could refashion these words into a mantra reminiscent of the phrase coined by James Carville in 1992, lead strategist for President Bill Clinton: It's the relationships, stupid!

Exactly.

So, here's to relationships. Here's to what brings us together and holds us together—in any number of ways.

Here's to the ties that bind.

Grace and peace,
   ~J.A. Bouma • January 2022

STORY 1

CLEAN UP ON AISLE 6!

THREE. More. Hours. To. Go.

I sat nestled amidst a sea of plush pillows and heavy blankets smelling of my grandmother beneath a blazing fire at the center of a rug anchoring her vast living room watching the minutes tick by toward midnight on the elaborate 19th-century gold clock resting on the black-and-white veiny marble mantle—wishing to God I had a bottle of champagne to wash down the self-pity.

And a bottle of scotch. Might as well throw gin into the mix as well. And one of those beefy Harlequin men wrapped in vines, perhaps clinging a Corinthian column and smelling of opportunity. Anything to drown my sorrows and embarrassment at spending the last few hours of the year from hell with someone other than anyone else I could snog and shag and any other British term for anything but what I would be doing to now—the pitiful fact I was spending New Year's Eve with Granny.

Not that there was anything wrong with my grandmother. Loved her to pieces! Owed her my life. Literally, after adopting me when Mom and Dad died. But also all I had made of my life, all of who I was—the woman having paid my way through Harvard and handed me most of her fortune on top of the reins to her newspaper, the *Mill Creek Junction Guardian*. An overly pretentious name to the family business that had survived four generations of Nollands going clear back to the Junction's founding in 1876.

And there I was, swimming in a sea of mauve blankets complemented by taupe gold-tasseled plump pillows in a room that echoed with the ticking of my life.

I closed my eyes, pilling on the pillows and breathing in deeply, the spicy scent of burning wood and smoke filling my senses, along with the scent of vanilla from a collection of candles I had lit an hour ago. Not the best combo, but seemed good at the time.

How did I get to this point? Single and nearly forty, with nothing to do the night closing out the year? I should be at Times Square, wrapped in the arms of said Harlequin model rippling with chords of muscle while dipping me back just as the ball dropped and laying one on me, hot and heavy.

I took in a breath, heart picking up pace and feeling warm now—whether from the fire or fantasy, I wasn't sure. All I knew was that I was all alone—no one calling, no one texting; no one *to* call, no one *to* text—in a town I would never in my wildest imaginations have thought I'd settle down in, lying on my Granny's floor without a bottle of champagne on New Year's Eve.

Yep. This was my life...

And that wasn't even touching on the fact it was the one-year anniversary from when I discovered Todd cheating on me. He was perfect too. Smart and sweet, fit and healthy. On a partnership track at his law firm, owned his own house, even picked up his clothes and put them in the hamper on top of putting the toilet lid back down after taking care of business!

Again, perfect.

Aside from the side dish he'd been enjoying while his main entrée had been clueless for months...

Could really use that champagne right about now!

"Tracy, dear," Granny said, her sturdy voice with a New England lilt echoing throughout the vast space.

I bolted upright at the sound. Mostly out of wide-eyed embarrassment that Granny had interrupted my pity-party!

"Ooh, so sorry! Did I startle you?"

I ran a hand through my hair, catching my breath and throwing up a giggle. "Just a tad, but it's alright." I scooted to the side to make space and patted the mound of pillows. "Here, Granny. Join me by the fire. Less than three hours until the new year, now."

"Thank you kindly, dear, but I'm an old sack of bones who's no longer fit for such extravagant affairs!"

I smiled at the idea that staying up to midnight was an extravagant affair. But I suppose when I'm 90, I'll feel the same.

"You're not feeling poorly, I hope," I said, settling back into my pile.

"No, no. Just ready to hit the sack. You alright? Do you need anything?"

"A bottle of champagne and a man would be nice."

A good man...

She laughed, a high and heady noise that soared throughout the vast room. The sound that carried me through adolescence, kept me going through young adult-hood and beyond.

"Don't we all! But sorry, dear. Two strikes out on both counts!"

"Yay me..."

Granny padded toward me, hair down and curling past her shoulders, wearing pink silk jammies with her spectacles hanging around her neck from a solid-gold chain. Arms open with the hug that had carried me through it all.

I stood, opening up and leaning into her embrace.

She whispered, "Happy New Year, dear. I predict grand things are in store for you in the coming months."

My eyes suddenly pricked with emotion, my throat giving way to the same. I didn't share my grandmother's optimism, but I would never let her know.

Swallowing hard and quickly wiping my eyes, I leaned out of the embrace with a smile. "Our life is the creation of our mind, after all." It was a favorite saying of Granny's.

Her eyes widened, along with her mouth. Then she grabbed my face with both hands and kissed my forehead. "Exactly, my dear! Now, enjoy your night and I'll see you on the morrow."

Granny left the way she came, offering a wave as she shuffled toward the spiral staircase.

"Good night," I said, waving as she disappeared into the darkness, her footfalls up the marble stairs fading.

My face fell, and I slumped along with it back to the floor. Lying down, I closed my eyes again, sinking deeper into the sea of plush pillows and blankets. More ticking, more self-pity.

Then I snapped my eyes open and sat upright. "What the hell am I doing? I'm a 21st-century woman, dammit. I've got agency! If I want champagne, by golly I'll get one. And a Harlequin man!"

I jolted to my feet and dashed toward the garage. Grabbing my keys and purse along the way, I wrapped myself in Granny's bleach-white fur coat, slipped on a pair of ruby stilettos, and sliped a pair of chunky black sunglasses into my coat pocket—giving not a lick I was still wearing my own pink jammies but also realizing in that moment I was all matchy-matchy with my ninety-year-old Granny! Yay me...

Screw it. If there was one woman I'd want to match, it's Granny.

I headed out to my car, hoping for a win, the night cold and crisp, sky wide and open, the waning night still bursting with possibilities—what was left of it, anyway.

Surely, Meyer's General will have some sort of bubbly for the night. Heck, good ol' Freddy Meyer might have a Harlequin hunk stashed in the storeroom!

A girl can hope.

And hope is what New Year's Eve is all about.

———

Max's Place was bangin', if Max didn't say so himself! Though he was a bit preoccupied at the moment to notice what he'd been relishing just a few minutes ago.

The joint was smelling of onions and peppers, frying beef and fish, a little garlic and saffron thrown in for good measure. Marvin and the Gang were doing their thing on stage, the headliner himself working his Hammond organ like it was nobody's business, with his backups strumming that bass and *rat-a-tat-tatting* those drums and ringin' in the new year with that trumpet. Convos and laughter, fueled by more booze than the Junction knew what to do with. Oh yeah, it was gonna be one kick-ass night!

Now if only he could find that champagne...

"Burt!" Max yelled, poking his noggin' up from behind

the bar—his bar, in his bar. Or more accurately, Max's Place.

Nothing but the sound of sizzling meat and sharpened knives chopping up salads and muffled curses was my response.

Not that he minded too bad. Meant Burt and his crew were hard at work feeding the Junction on one of Max's busiest days. The only thing that would enhance the sound-track was the *cha-ching* of cash registers throwing up their hidey-ho and good-day-to-yas! But he knew most people paid with credit cards, so he'd have to settle for the whis-pering slide of plastic. If he cocked his head just right, he could almost hear it above the din of the packed crowd and Marven working the organ up on stage like it was nobody's business. Simon & Garfunkel got it wrong. The sound of success was where it was at!

Which was interrupted by a sharp scream, followed by the door to the kitchen flying open with a slap, and the bassy blast of a fire extinguisher wielded by Burt himself!

"What the hot Hades!" Max yelled, scrambling back as a white cloud of fire-squelching agent burst into the kitchen.

"Sorry, boss," Burt said, Max's faithful burly bald cook slick with sweat and short on excuses. "Had a little incident with the grill."

"I can see that!"

"Don't worry, all is cool."

Waited for the ear-splitting shrill of the fire alarm, but all seemed in order. Which was either a good thing or a fire-code violation waiting to happen. He'd have to look into that next year—which was tomorrow!

That would have to wait. Because what he needed in that moment was to find a damn bottle of champagne—or twelve, considering the bar was plumb out. Which didn't seem right.

"Now that I've got ya..." Max said, resuming his rummaging through boxes and cases of booze under the bar. "You seen anymore champagne? Could've sworn I ordered a whole mess load, but we're plumb out!"

"Pretty sure I brought up the last of it half an hour ago," Sheila said, Max's faithful server who basically kept his head on and kept his bar humming along.

"What?" Max sank to his knees as Burt went back into the kitchen to resume his post, pushing aside a few metal kegs and finding nothing more than mouse traps with shriveled-up cheese.

"Don't tell me we've run out..." Sheila moaned, her blond curls bobbin on slight shoulders as she popped the tops off two bottles of beer and stuffed ice down the gullet of a glass. Filling it with water, she continued "I've got two tables waiting on four glasses each!"

"We must be going through it like water..." Max said, standing with a frown.

"Or like—champagne," she said with a wink. "Folks wanna celebrate the dawning of a new year after the hell we've been through. Went through eight bottles myself the past hour, and imagine the other gals have done the same."

"But how do you ring in the new year without champagne?"

She loaded her beers and water on a tray and answered, "Same way you do ringing in the new year without a hot date." Then she left, shouting behind her "You don't!"

He shouted after her, "Well, I've got neither, so what does that say about me?"

Sheila didn't look back, getting lost in the crowds tending to her tables.

Not good, Max Blade...

Throwing a towel across his shoulder, he went to fold his arms, Gideon O'Donnell and his new fiance Annabelle Kirkland sat down at the bar.

"What do you want?" he snapped, mind whirlin' and turnin' and doin' somersaults trying to work out how to solve his dilemma.

"Happy New Year to you too, Max," Gideon said, "Sheesh."

Max frowned. "Sorry. Things just go a bit....tenuous."

He threw his date a frown of his own. "Sounds...Dickensian."

"Big word for a small-town lawyer. What can I get ya?"

He chuckled. "A bottle of champagne and two glasses."

Max's cheeks flushed hot. "Ya just had to ask, didn't ya?"

Gideon threw Annabelle a raised brow. "Was it something I said?"

Grabbing his Carhartt jacket draped across a stool behind the bar, Max stormed off, shouting, "I'll be back in thirty with your bloomin' bottle of champagne!"

Squeezing between Mayor Goodall and Chief Roller as Marvin and the Gang struck up some jazz number Max remembered Gramps playing a time or two, he stormed off through the back door, cool air a welcomed relief from the hot and stuffy barroom.

Not that he was complaining. Hot and stuffy meant people packed like sardines—and their wallets. Judging by the tab tally so far that night, they were opening them with abandon. Made sense after such a crap show of a year.

He pushed through the back door and was slapped in the face with a biting December 31st night. An easy breeze carried along the dueling scents of chimney smoke and fried food billowing from his exhausts under a clear, star-filled sky.

Reaching the Golden Nugget, his affectionately named Plymouth Breeze—because everyone needs a junker at some point in their life, so it might as well be a Breeze—Max breathed in deeply and slid inside, firing up the beast and wishing to the New Year's Eve gods for success.

Didn't take long before Max was pulling into Meyer's General, the parking lot lit up with those crazy-ass newfangled LED lights that made his eyes bug out. Suppose the added high-wattage helped deter any would-be miscreants and ne'er-do-well roaming the lot with ill intent. Bothered eyes his something fierce, though.

So he threw the Golden Nugget into 'Park', threw on a black duster he kept in his backseat for such a time as these, then shut 'er down and darted through the lot on toward destiny.

The innards of the town grocery store weren't much better. Good ol' Freddy must have upgraded his lights in the last week. Maybe changed some bulbs or finally got around to cleaning the light covers that made him near well stop patronizing the joint. Cracked light coverings with dead flies and splattered with dressing and soda from careless customers made him lose his lunch a time or twelve.

But Max pressed on through the cramped space sparse with people and curiously low on foodstuff. Made sense, he supposed, given it was the last day of the year and Junction folk liked to party-hardy.

Negotiating past a bin of green beans and russet potatoes, he hustled past an empty meat case and rounded the aisles counting down from one to six—checking his watch and throwing up a shriek.

Two hours left to the ten-minute countdown. Time to kick it into high gear.

So Max did, trotting now with a bit of Pine-Sol flaring up as he hustled across the scuffed floor. He rounded the end-cap of party poppers into the aisle—

When he spotted it. Right before he spotted her.

Truth be told, he spotted her first. A cougar as old as Mama rounding the same aisle dressed in a white coat that would give Cruella Devil a run for her money, especially with those ruby-red stilettos and dark sunglasses.

Then he spotted it.

The single bottle of champagne sitting all innocent like on the center shelf of the beer and wine aisle.

She stopped, standing still and stiff, seemingly eyeing the same bottle of—

Max gasped. It hit him that she was eyeing the same bottle of champagne!

Not good, Max Blade...

Without warning, she took off, hiking up that fur coat of hers, those sexy stilettos flaring up an echoey *click-click-click* on toward destiny.

My destiny!

"Hey!" Max shouted, running after the cougar. "That's my champagne!"

Then he channeled his high school track-star moves, sprinting to intercept the goods.

———

There you are...

Spotting the bottle from across the aisle, I darted for the solution to my New Year's Eve problems, adjusting my sunglasses to shield my eyes from that godawful lighting.

Either I was getting old, or Mr. Meyer redid his lighting. Hoped for the latter; probably the former.

My stilettos threw up an echoey *click-click-click* across Meyer's expertly waxed floor a little slick for my ruby shoes. Got my champagne. Now all I needed was that Harlequin man, cords of muscle rippling with ill intent and heart bursting with the kind of love that would sweep me off my feet.

I snorted a laugh on my approach. "Fat chance in Mill Creek..." All the good fellas I remember from high school were either in jail or dead, married or near there, or—

"Hey, that's my champagne!"

I stopped cold and spread out my arms for balance, my right foot skidding an inch. Snapping my head toward the voice, I saw the perp at the far end of the aisle.

Guy had on one of those cowboy coats with matching black cowboy hat sitting on a messy bed of blond locks. Had to adjust my glasses again to shield my aging eyes from the fluorescent lights to get a better look at him, but—

I squinted for a better look, then startled. "Is that Max Blade?"

And was he tearing toward the only bottle of champagne left in Mill Creek Junction?

"Not on your life, pal..."

Hiking up Granny's fur coat, I took the little weasel up on his challenge and tore down the aisle myself, all modesty flying out the window with my silk jammies flapping in the breeze of Meyer's General HVAC—which sent up a very uninvited cold breeze up my backside—my ruby stilettos rapping a typewriter beat telling Max to back off!

Except he didn't, but I didn't care how I looked.

I. Needed. The. Bubbly!

It was going to be close, Max hiking up his legs and

moving his arms like a crazy person. But I was matching him hike for hike, closing the cap and homing in on the bubbly.

My bubbly!

"Not on my dead body, cougar!" Max shouted, face red and that ridiculous cowboy hat taking a tumble with the breeze of his gait.

Cougar? I looked at my coat and shoes and adjusted my glasses. How old does he think I am?

Didn't matter. I was close now. But it would be a photo finish.

If Granny could see me now...

Almost—

Max dove for the bottle, Fred Meyer's expertly waxed floors offering just the helping hand I needed. Poor guy literally slid face-first across the floor toward the shelf, reaching for the bottle.

Right before I snatched it from his grubby little hands.

"*Arg!*" Max cried out as he slid into the empty shelf with a *smack*. The force of it all threw up a surprising rippling effect across the shelving, rattling the whole empty structure so that it wobbled back and forth.

All the while I stood dumbly looking at the thing, not knowing what to make of it.

Or what to do.

Max did, springing to his knees and shouting, "Get 'ur boots a walkin', cougar!"

Right before he grabbed me by the waist and pushed me out of the way—the pair of us tumbling to the floor in a heap. Lost my purse in the process, and my glasses.

Just as the shelving unit fell forward and crashed into the bottles of beer neatly arrayed on a complementary set of shelves.

The packs of Miller and Bud didn't have a chance. Not that they should have had one anyway—the 12-packs and 6-packs collapsing in a heaping pile.

Sending a malty, hoppy, frothy geyser as pressurized cans exploded and glass bottles crashed, a river of pilsner spilling across the floor.

"Not good, Max Blade..." he moaned on top of me, glancing over his shoulder. "Clean up on aisle six, I guess."

Then he looked at me, blue eyes wide and panicked, that head of hair all mad scientist. "Tracy Nolland?"

I put on a sheepish grin. "The one and only."

"You're no cougar," Max said, face twisting up in confusion.

I frowned. "You think? Get off me, Max!"

He scrambled off as I searched for my glasses, then realized they were the reason for the pain in my left butt cheek. I sat up and retrieved them. Just as I thought: cracked.

"Is it safe?" Max asked in a panicked rush, looming over me.

I looked up at him. "Is what safe?"

He sighed and rolled his eyes. "The champagne!"

Now my cheek cheeks reddened with rage, eyes narrowing with the same. "Would you help me up already?" I snapped at him, trying to keep my legs closed to maintain some sort of lady-like dignity.

"Oh, right. Here, let me..." Max scrambled toward me, holding out a hand and helping me stand, his forearms bulging through his Carhartt jacket in a way I hadn't noticed before. Between those arms and that jacket, those eyes and that tousled blond hair—and that baby face left-over from our days at Mill Creek High...suddenly my cheeks flushed with something entirely unexpected.

Not Harlequin level, but still...

He helped me up, and I thanked him. Then I pulled out the goods he was looking for, careful not to reveal anything more underneath.

His eyes widened and mouth went with it. "Come to papa..."

He reached for the bottle, his hand brushing mine as he wrapped a manly paw around the bottle's neck.

A fluttering wave of—something ran from my heart to my toes!

Which was entirely unexpected.

Wasn't sure if it was out of sheer shock from the man's brazenness, trying to swipe the bottle from me like that. Or...something else I hadn't experienced in over a year.

No way. Not Max Blade!

The guy owned a bar and I was the chief guardian of Junction news—literally, chief editor of Granny's *Guardian*! I was raised on the westside of Main Street; he north of the tracks. I was a Harvard-educated, urban professional, and Max a small-town, high-school dropout. What was I thinking?

What would people say?

What would Granny say?

But...boy, oh, boy—that touch, that jolting wave. And that smell flaring up from that jacket of his! Something salty, something spicy, something—dare I say...sexy?

Max yanked at the bottle now, snapping my out of delusions and back to the task at hand.

Keeping that bottle!

So I yanked it back with more force than he probably imagined I could muster, stuffing it back inside Granny's fur coat.

"Whoa, She-Ra Turner," Max exclaimed with a laugh, putting up his hands and flashing a set of perfectly white teeth—sending up another fluttering wave—before adding: "Where'd you get those cannons?"

"Max!" I shouted, shuffling back and heaving a breath.

"What? That's my champagne!"

"Whatever, I got to it first, and you know it!"

"But—But—But I saved your life," he stammered.

"No thanks to your fancy footwork!" I bit back. "Wouldn't have needed saving had you not banged into those set of shelves."

"I had no choice! You were going all Paula Radcliffe on me."

"Who?"

"Only the best British long-distance runner to—oh, never mind. Just hand it over already!"

"No way! And why do you need it, anyway? You own the Junction's only bar!"

He took a breath and sighed, running a hand through those locks of his. "Yeah, well, I ran out."

"You ran out?" A giggle slipped through my lips, but the look he gave me made me regret it.

"Yeah, I know. Impeccable timing. But why are you stalking through Freddy's joint—" he paused to check his watch, eyes widening. "An hour before midnight!"

"Because I needed champagne, why else?"

He scoffed. "Why, you and your date already blew through the first two bottles. And why isn't he here, anyway? Not a chivalrous fella, if he's sending his chickadee for alcohol run an hour before midnight."

"Hey! I'm a 21st-century woman. I make my own alcohol run an hour before midnight, thank you very much."

"Oh, I hear you roar..."

"And—And—And besides," I stammered, "I don't need a man to celebrate the new year. I'm—I'm...independent!"

Didn't sound so convincing, but I was getting irritated at the back and forth. And confused. What was going on here? Why wasn't I just storming off and paying for my legit right to the bottle? After all, I got there first! Max had no right to it—

Max...

There was that damn fluttering wave again. Running from head to toe.

"Alright, sassafras, simmer. But how we gonna get out of this one? After all, we've got a Faustian dilemma on our hands, here."

I furrowed my brow. "Don't you mean Faustian bargain?"

"Same difference."

"And what am I trading? I got the goods. You didn't. Case close!"

He sighed and threw his arms up in the air in a huff. "Look, Tracy, I've got a bar full of unruly patrons who'll tar and feather me and string me up a bean pole if I don't come back with more champagne." He got down on his knees now, slapping his hands together and adding, "So I'm beggin' ya, sassafras, hand over that bottle."

Had to laugh; almost did. The guy looked so—cute, on the floor like that? Felt a bit sorry for the fella. I took a breath and gathered my wits. The bottle was mine, and I needed it more than him.

Especially that night...

Should have walked then, but before I knew it, I was blurting out: "Tell you what. I'll play you for it."

"Play me for it?"

I shrugged. Why not. "Yeah. A round of this-or-that."

He stood, face twisted up with confusion. "This-or-whatchamacallit?"

"This-or-that. We each give an answer to a pair of contrasts, and the best one gets a point. Like Mac or PC."

Max scoffed. "That's an easy one. It's neither. Linux, all the way."

Wow, what a nerd. Which made him all the more mysterious!

"Clearly you get the idea. So, what do you say? Best of three?"

He folded his arms. "Best of five, and you've got yourself a deal."

One end of my mouth curled upward, and now I let the bottle come out from hiding.

"Deal."

———

All Max could think was: What the heck am I doing, negotiating with this She-ra Turner terrorist?

Thought the bottle should be his. He needed it more, anyway! Surely her Granny had a whole cellar of them things. He was just trying to get by, keep his people happy, keep his joint alive for another month. She was flush with cash and had that real cougar of hers to keep her nice and fat and happy.

Well, not fat. No way was Tracy Nolland fat. No way, José! God almighty was she a hot little vixen...even if she was wearing her granny's fur coat. And *a* fur coat. Was partial to fine, furry friends, tithing ten percent of his profits to his animal-cause of choice.

But man...that jolting wave of twitterpation when he brushed her hand grabbing for the bottle. Kept a tight grip just to keep the twitterpated connection—didn't want to let go!

Tracy cleared her throat. "Shall we get to it?"

Max nodded and grinned. "Ladies first."

She threw him a grin in return. "Alright. First round: beer or wine?"

"*Psht*. That's easy. Both."

She laughed. "Good answer."

"And you?" he said, leaning in.

Tracy held up the bottle of champagne, bringing it to her cheeks with a smile.

Max frowned. "I ain't never getting that bottle, am I?"

"Not on your life."

"Then what about on my children's?"

She twisted up her face. "You don't have kids!"

"I might someday," he said with a shrug. Pointing to the champagne, he continued, "and that there bottle could be the difference between a nice-sized nest-egg inheritance from Max's Place. Gotta keep the customers happy to keep my coffers filled to the brim."

"Don't you mean your non-existent kiddo's inheritance coffers?"

"Same difference."

"Alright, new topic—"

"Wait, wait, wait," Max said, putting up a hand. "Who won?"

Tracy shrugged. "Why, me of course."

Max went to retort but snapped his yapper. Best to keep the objections for when it mattered.

"Alright, new topic," he said instead. "Detroit Lions or Ohio Buckeyes."

She scoffed. "That's not even a contest. Buckeyes."

He frowned. "Yeah, pretty much."

"Guess we're tied, then."

"Guess so." Max clapped his hands together and rubbed

them, liking the game. "Alright, I got the next mix. Donut or scone."

"What kind of this-or-that contrast is that?"

"Just give your answer."

"Donut. Hands down."

"Hmm, I would have taken you as a scone kind of girl."

Tracy crossed her arms and leaned back. "What's that supposed to mean?"

Max brought a hand to his chin, feeling like he was treading on thin ice.

"You know, you're more of the urbane sort than the working-man stiff."

"And the urbane sort can't like donuts?"

"It's not that the urbane sort don't like donuts. It's that they prefer their tea and crumpets to coffee and donuts."

"I thought we were talking about scones!"

"Whatever. Your point, because I liked your answer."

"Gee, thanks."

"But apparently I've got a lot to learn about Tracy Nolland."

She grinned. "You have no idea, pal."

Max suppressed a smile now. I bet.

"My turn," Tracy said. "Rolling Stones or Beatles."

"Definitely Led Zeppelin. Another point for me," he said with a grin.

"That wasn't an option!"

Max shrugged. "I made it an option."

"You can't do that!"

"Why not? What, are you the this-or-that police?"

Now she scoffed. "Actually, yes. It was my bloomin' game!"

"Yeah, yeah, yeah," Max complained. "Whatever. But where does it leave us on this cockamamie game of yours?"

"Looks like we're tied."

"Guess so."

"What shall it be, then? Game winning point you know."

The pair stood under the blinding fluorescent lights in silence, considering the final question. Some store clerk was starting to mop the mess up behind them, but they paid him no attention. Didn't even realize he was there, they were so zoned into one another.

Until Tracy snapped her fingers. "I got it."

"What's that."

"Favorite show. Between—" She put a finger to her mouth, then smiled. "Survivor and Lost."

Max muttered, "I think the 20th century just called and wants its shows back..."

Tracy put a hand on her hips and frowned.

"Sorry! But that's a no brainer anyway," Max said.

He went to answer when she put up a finger. "Let's say it together, alright? Because no wrong answer on that one."

"So you say..."

Tracy frowned, then counted: "One, two, three—"

'*Survivor!*' the pair said in unison.

"What?" Max said with marvel.

"For real?" Tracy said with matched amazement.

"You're a Survivor chick?"

"I've been watching it since Richard and Rudy and that she-devil woman."

"Sue Hawk." Max said.

Tracy laughed. "Ahh, yes. The black widow. Granny and I've been watching it with from day one. She and I would order pizza, and she would drain half a bottle of wine before the immunity challenge."

"And you'd drain the rest by tribal council?"

She shrugged. "Maybe..."

Max laughed. "Little Tracy Nolland. Captain of the cheerleading team from Mill Creek High, journalist extra-ordinaire from Big City, USA, who inherited her grandma's small-town newspaper—a raving survivor fan. Who would have thunk?"

Tracy shrugged. "What can I say? I'm like an onion with untold layers, just waiting to be peeled back with discovery."

"Apparently!" the man exclaimed, looking at her with new eyes. Almost like she was a normal person, someone who wasn't entirely out of his league. Someone he'd love to peel...

"Alright, answer me this," she said, clapping her hands together. "If you had one Survivor spirit animal, who would it be?"

Max twisted up his face in confusion. "You mean like, who am I most like, on the show?"

"Something like that."

He crossed his arms and looked off for a moment, then snapped his fingers. "Gotta go with Ozzy."

"Really? That boy wonder who could shimmy up a coconut tree, right?"

"Hands down. Guy swam like some merman and stocked his tribe with fish for days!"

"Sucked at winning, though."

"Oh, come on! He spanked 'em all at challenges!"

"I mean the game. You know, for a million bucks. Didn't he have like three shots, and lost them all."

Max frowned. "Suppose you've got a point there."

"That's funny," Tracy said, shifting to one leg. "I took you more as a Johnny-fair-play guy."

"What? The dude who used his dead grandma as a sympathy card?"

"Fake dead grandma. Or I guess, his grandma was real, but her death was fake."

"Even worse!"

"I don't know. I thought it was a pretty good move. Something I'd do."

"Really?" Max said. That was unexpected.

Tracy shrugged. "Maybe."

"Interesting..." The layers kept getting better and better! "Well, then, who's your Survivor spirit animal?"

Tracy took a breath and looked off, answering, "Sandra. Definitely Sandra."

"Ahh, Ms. Diaz-Twine. The Queen, herself."

She laughed. "You know her last name? And her nickname?"

Max reddened, his cheeks growing warm and heat rising up the back of his neck. "Yeah, maybe...But it fits. I mean, Sandra as your spirit survivor, or animal, or whatever."

One end of her mouth curled upward. "Really? How so?"

He took a breath, then let it fly.

"Well, for starters, you're a genuine 21st-century sort of gal aren't ya? Smart and successful, independent and capable all on your own. You're funny and fun. A little stand-offish in that urbane sort of way." Tracy raised a brow at that, but Max recovered: "And I mean that in a good way! Like you don't take crap from no one—least of all guys like me." She seemed to like that one. "Then of course you're dropped dead gorgeous. A little odd in the fashion department, but I can work with it."

Tracy giggled, putting a hand to her mouth. Max grinned, feeling like he hadn't felt since high school.

———

I felt a rising emotion seize my throat and eyes. What was coming over me? It was the sweetest thing anyone has said to me. Even more than Todd, but this time it sounded like Max meant it. Every word.

But I it was stupid, totally stupid of me to find comfort in his affirmations. I mean, it's Max Blade! And I was totally rebounding here, knowing the anniversary of my serendipitous ending to my engagement was priming me to be swept off my feet. In Meyer's General, of all places!

I swallowed and batted away the emotion in my eyes, recovering and glancing at my watch.

Only ten minutes till the ball drop!

"What's wrong?" he asked.

I took in a startled breath, the man having inched toward me with a face that registered concern. Chivalrous, even. Like he might reach in to comfort me at my sudden turn—which was the last thing I needed!

So I held up my wrist, pointing at my watch. "No way we're going to make it now. Almost midnight."

Max scoffed. "You've never seen me drive."

"Oh, yes, I have!" I exclaimed.

"What's that supposed to mean!"

"It means, either that Golden Nugget of yours has a turbocharged engine on that Plymouth piece of junk, or you've got a lead foot that'll get you in trouble before long."

Cheeks reddening, he offered a nervous giggle. "Suppose I should put that on the ol' new year's resolution list, ehh?"

"Perhaps."

Max nodded toward the champagne bottle still firmly in my grasp. "Well, then, what are we gonna do with that? Can't very well let it go to waste, now can we?"

I let a wry grin spread across my face. "Might as well pop the top now."

Face brightening, he leaned in and whispered, "Is that legal?"

"Probably not. But..." I glanced around, the store clerk having finished and left, then added: "I don't think anyone's going to find out. After all, it's almost midnight. On New Year's Eve. Whose dumb or pathetic enough to be trolling down aisle six at Meyer's General?"

Max raised a knowing brow.

"Alright, don't answer that." I started unwrapping the foil from the bottle top.

He glanced at his watch. "Whoa! We've been jawing it up for almost two hours now!"

"Time flies when you're having fun, they say." I was working the cork but having trouble.

"Here, let me..." Max went to take it, but I held firm.

Raising one end of my mouth, I said, "You're not going to run off with the goods, now are you?"

He grinned. "Wouldn't dream of it."

I held the bottle a beat, and his gaze—that fluttering jolt returning, from head to toe! I almost kept it from him, our two eyes locked on one another, just to keep the connection going—and that flutter a fluttering! But I relented, holding it by the neck and passing it along.

His hand came in and brushed against my own, his fingers sliding across my skin as he settled on the bottle's girth and eyes keeping our connection. A sudden heat raced up and down my neck at it all again, and I let go.

He took the bottle and started wrenching the cork this way and that. Little bugger was jammed in their tight. Had to throw it against his ribcage for leverage, it was stuck down there so tight.

"Careful," I warned. "You're gonna shake it."

"Don't worry, sassafras. I'm a professional."

I backed off, letting the man work. Soon enough he wrenched the cork out with a *pop*.

"Houston, we've got a problem," Max said.

"What's that?"

"No glasses."

"Who cares? Let's just tip it back on cue."

Max furrowed his brow. "What, like swap spit?"

Gladly. Didn't say that, of course. Perhaps I should have.

Instead, I said, "Why not?"

His mouth dropped at first, face unsure of the turn. But then he whispered what I was unable to, or afraid to, or something: "Gladly."

We stood still for a moment, my breath growing shallow with each passing second. Hadn't felt this way in ages. Which was odd, because it was over Max Blade!

I know, super pretentious and petty, judgy and just plain scummy. But it was true. Probably because of Granny, drilling into me to marry a proper man, from a proper background. With money and position and connections.

Believe me, I tried that. And all it left me with was a New Year's Eve at Granny's all alone without a bottle of champagne!

And yet...

Look where that got me.

"Hello...."

I blinked, then again, coming out from my trance.

Max smiled and smacked his wrist with two fingers. "Tick tock."

I took a breath and smiled, then looked at my watch. Startling!

"Oh! I guess so. Sixty seconds to the new year."

"There is a God! After this crazy-ass year—I'd say the collective humanity needs it."

I nodded. "Agreed."

Then I brought my wrist up for us to view, the second hand rounding the thirty-second bend now. The two of us smiled, anticipation welling like it hadn't since I was a teenager.

Max grabbed my wrist. "Twenty seconds now!"

And that fluttering wave flared up again, growing and piling and crescendoing—a new set of flush attacking my cheeks, and heat blooming at my neck.

I took a breath and eased it out, smiling. "Only a few seconds now."

"On three..." he said.

We cried out together, right there in aisle six of Meyer's General: '*Three. Two. One!*'

He handed me the bottle first and I took a swig. It was heaven, the bubbles tickling my nose and the apricot and key-lime nectar sending my tastebuds dancing.

Handing Max the bottle, he took it. His hand brushed mine again, sending up that fluttering jolt. Priming me for what I wanted next.

Hoped he did too, but who cared?

The man closed his eyes and wrapped his lips around the bottle's mouth, my heart racing now and cheeks flushing at the sight—wishing it were me.

Getting ready for it *to* be me.

He tossed back a swig and chugged a few gulps of the

bubbly like the pro he was. Then came up for air—but I wouldn't let him.

Throwing caution to the wind, and prim-and-proper upbringing that would surely scandalize Granny, I grabbed his face with both hands and latched onto his lips with mine.

Before long, we were necking like two people half our age. And even then, half that!

Then it was over.

I pulled away, opening my eyes, my face on fire and lips tingling from it all.

He smiled and sighed with pleasure, "Happy New Year to me..."

"Amen," I sighed as well.

Right there in the middle of the beer and wine aisle of Meyer's General. Me and Max. New Year's Eve. Never saw that coming.

Boy, did he call it the first time: Clean up on aisle six is right!

Max downed what seemed like half the bottle. He passed it off it me and I finished the rest.

"Suppose we should pay for this," I said, holding up the empty bottle.

He grabbed my other hand. "Together."

I looked down at them, all wrapped together. The fluttering wave was more like a ripple now. Perhaps I'd grown accustomed to his touch. Imagine that.

Then I caught his eyes, throwing him a wry grin. "Cash or check?"

"Charge..." he said in this weirdly sexy voice. Didn't know what that implied, but I got the drift. In a Max Blade sort of way.

"Come on, then," I said. "Let's blow this joint."

And we did. The new year that was still a blank slate, and we started filling it that night. Or morning, or whatever.

Suppose the old Scottish new year song is right: Old acquaintances shouldn't be forgot. Not a pint cup, but a cup of kindness will do.

And a cup of love.

The year was looking up already.

With a view from aisle six from Meyer's General. In Mill Creek Junction.

Imagine that.

STORY 2

A STRAND OF THREE CORDS

THE BUILDING for my law practice was sweltering by the time I arrived, the dead-of-August heat pressing in like crazy and thickened by midnight storms. Did our air conditioner fritz out? If it did...what a way to start the day. Add to that oversleeping after preparing all night for trial against Annabelle Kirkland, yet again, and something knocking around under the Audi hood—and, well, it was going to be one of those days.

At least the hallway was smelling of coffee. Not the tin-can kind, mind you, but the coffee shop variety, the vents from Starbucks next door working about as well as they usually did, but probably compounded by the heat. Not that I minded. On top of the grande triple-shot Americano I was holding, the strong coffee scent alone should do the trick to smacking me upside the head and waking me up, the air probably laced with caffeine.

And at least my name was on the door to the office.

O'Donnell and Associates.

I stood in front of it holding my white grande cup bearing the green Siren, one end of my mouth curling upward at the sight of that gold ink set inside thick black edges in a sort of old-school banker-like serif typeface that harkened back to Mill Creek Junction's early days, the text set against frosted glass and arched with just the right amount of curve, a judges gavel set underneath in a sort of exclamation point that emphasized the justice I offered my clients.

Scratch that. *Brought* my clients.

Not so bad of a day after all.

I credit Dad with the whole thing. And not just the graphic arts job that rivaled the best in the business.

After graduating law school, I'd hemmed and hawed over next steps. Georgetown Law where I'd spent the last three years slaving away in DC wasn't the top law school around. But it wasn't the worst either, tying for fifteenth with Cornell and Vanderbilt and University of Texas-Austin. Could have gotten me into some decent lobbying firms in the city, even a banking gig up the East Coast. None of it sounded appealing. I'd even caught a dose of Potomac Fever for a spell, putting out a few feelers out on Capitol Hill, but politics made my stomach turn. And I thought I was better built for solo work anyhow.

When I brought up my misgivings and trepidations with Dad, he suggested I start a private practice back in the Junction. I literally laughed out loud at the suggestion. Taking the solo-practitioner plunge was attractive, but I'd vowed never to return to West Michigan after fleeing for grad school. Yet there was a ring to his suggestion that seemed true, seemed alright, seemed meant to be. Wasn't much of a praying man any more, so I spent a weekend along the Appalachian Trail hiking and camping and weighing it all. And when I made it back down the trail to my Honda hatchback, the plan had been hatched, so to speak.

When I finally made the decision to come back home to the Junction, Dad put his graphic design know-how to work and fixed me up the set of shingles anchoring my front door. It had started as a hobby a decade back before it turned into side hustle after he lost his job at the farm during the '08-'09 recession. Which lasted another few years before they were able to hire him back. Thankfully, Ma had her nursing job at Mercy General, but things had been tight a while, and his side gig had made up part of the difference.

And there that difference was, staring my barely awake eyes in the face, sweat beading down my forehead now as I stood grasping the burnished bronze doorknob that felt surprisingly cool to the touch, considering the August hell-fires that had hovered in the wake of last night's storm. Where was a polar vortex when you needed—

The door suddenly opened.

And Lizzy screamed something fierce. Which sent me jumping back with a startled yell. And then Reggie joined in the fun behind her.

Then she lunged forward and smacked me in the chest with a manilla folder, nearly sending my grande triple-shot Americano to the scuffed wood floor below.

"What the hell are you doing creeping up on us like that!" she said before she gave way into a giggle. "Nearly scared the pants off me."

"Creeping up? I own the place!"

"Rent, more like it," Reggie corrected with that deep baritone voice that was so effective in court but not what I needed coming in late and hot and frightened myself nearly pantsless. "Which apparently don't count for much, since it's hotter than an Easy Bake Oven and we don't got no air!"

I frowned and shoved past the pair, taking my triple-shot Americano and memories with me into the office in the back, which wasn't saying much. I shouted back: "Don't worry, I'll call the landlord and straighten things out!"

My practice was really just two walls slapped together to separate the main area from my own humble work abode, with two windows looking out into the larger space of carpet the shade of mint Listerine from another century ago, walls white and blank and begging for some love with two dented wooden desks shedding their stain from sometime last century where Reggie and Lizzy slaved away for far less than what I made, which wasn't saying much.

I closed the door behind with a thud and set down my drink on a desk piled high with manilla folders spilling bent and misshapen papers. At least it all was shaded by pulled blinds, but what it shaded wasn't much better. The same century-ago wood desk bowing under the weight of too much work, a laptop anchoring a corner from back in college and a few thick cloth-over-board books fraying at the edges, the heat hovering with the same menacing molestation as the hallway and the outer room, but with far more ill intent. It was as if the hot humid air was clawing its way into my mouth and esophagus and lungs, it was so bad.

I loosened my tie and unbuttoned the top of my shirt, wishing to the Great Siren I would have sprung instead for an iced coffee. Or at least an iced version of the ten dollar concoction threatening to pass me out with every sip. Slumping into my well-worn leather chair, a gift from Dad when I opened up the joint, saying a workin' man needs a good chair, I popped the top to my Americano and closed my eyes, savoring the scent of coffee beans burnt and ground and brewed to perfection. Then I took a sip, the smooth yet spicy liquid burning my tongue in a way no Americano ever would in the fall.

Yeah, I definitely should have gone for an iced coffee.

There was a knock at the door.

I took another sip, then said, "Come in."

The door opened, and in walked Reggie and Lizzy. Actually, Lizzy first and then Reggie. She glanced back at him before pushing her long blond hair behind her ears, her mouth closed tight, lips pursed, eyes not making contact. For Reggie's part, his bald head was glistening under the pressure of the fritzed-out air conditioner and pursing his lips as well, not making eye contact.

Uh, oh...

I took another swig of the espresso and water concoction, then willed myself to take another, knowing I needed the jolt to get me through whatever was coming next.

Then I leaned back, the chair creaking in protest. "Hey, guys. What's up? If it's about the air conditioner, I was about to call up Tom right now and get things—"

"It ain't about that," Reggie interrupted, still looking at the floor.

Not good.

Another sip, another breath.

"Then what's this about?"

He stepped forward, not looking back at Lizzy and now fixing me with determined eyes. Guess it was his meeting, then.

"Gideon, we need to talk."

My heart sank, and bowels went with it, a cold dread spreading through my veins. His tone and timbre told me he meant business. And now Lizzy was looking at me too, face whiter than she'd been with lips still pursed.

Definitely not good.

I sat forward and took another sip, the liquid barely cooling under the oppressive heat, but I forced down the gulp, my tongue having formed a sort of callous under the amount of coffee I downed each day. Then I motioned for them to take a seat in a pair of crimson velour wood chairs. Before I realized they were piled high with more detritus of my law practice. More folders, more books, a stray brown paper lunch sack stained with grease.

I reddened and offered a sheepish smile, embarrassed at the mess. How had things gotten that bad? I stood and cleared a path, tossing the articles to the floor, *then* I motioned for them to sit.

They did, and I went back to my desk, mumbling: "It's hot as hades in here."

"Yeah, that's why we're here, my man," Reggie said, slumping down to my left. Lizzy followed, twisting up her long hair now behind her head and shoving a pencil through the pile to make it stay, then looking at her folded hands in her lap.

The look, combined with those fashionable thick black glasses she wore reminded me of a middle school English teacher I'd had. A shiver ran up my spine at the memory of her shrilly voice and those nails that dug into my arms whenever I misbehaved.

I cleared my throat and swallowed. "What do you mean? What does the heat have anything to do with why you're here?"

Reggie said nothing, glancing at Lizzy who looked up in time to meet his eyes. She cleared her throat now and offered, "It's Tom, Gideon. The landlord. He's...well, he's shut off our utilities."

The news thudded in the middle of the room like my shiny bowling league ball.

This is about utilities? And they're shut off?

I felt some relief at the news. Thought they were going to ask for a raise or something. Or worse: get up and walk out of my practice.

But then I glanced around my office, noticing for the first time the place was darker than usual, no lights on. My printer was off, as was the green banker's lamp sitting at the corner of my desk opposite my laptop. I didn't dare reach for the brass string hanging down to check it, because I knew what I'd find.

Nothing.

I almost grinned with the relief knowing utilities could be fixed. But their still-determined faces made me stuff my relief in a sack for now.

Because whatever was going down felt deeper than a dark, superheated office.

I swallowed and shifted in my chair, not returning to my coffee. Couldn't stomach adding to the adrenaline rush coursing through me now.

"I'll call Tom right now and see what's the matter. Surely there's a reasonable explanation—"

"We know what's the matter," Reggie said, interrupting again. He took a breath, drawing back his pursed lips as if mustering up the strength for what came next. "Rent's late. Again. Three months now, in fact. And not just late. Behind. Almost four months now, in fact. Which leaves Lizzy and me wondering what the hell is going on here."

Busted.

Now, any normal person might suck in a startled breath at the revelation, might offer a tell or reveal in the movement of their eyes or mouth or nose, a hand reaching for an ear or to rub their forehead or scratch the back of their head, their heart pounding and chest rising for more air and heat clawing up the back of their neck until it bloomed across their face with reddened revelation. Something to show weakness, to show they'd been caught or at least exposed.

Not me. I was Gideon O'Donnell. The best bloomin' attorney in Michigan. I knew how to hold a face.

And win.

I said nothing for a few seconds, then another set until I swallowed and leaned back, my mouth feeling like sandpaper and tasting of burnt coffee beans now from need of water. Both from the caffeine and the confrontation, not to mention the hot-as-hades heat threatening to keel me over.

Could the day get any worse?

I cleared my throat and said, "Where did you hear that?" About the only thing I could think of saying in response.

"Straight from the horse's mouth. I got off the phone with Tommy before you got in this morning."

I tried wetting my lips; it was no use. An unfortunate tell, but one I had to give because my mouth was a parched desert, on fire from the unexpected shift on top of being drained of hydration from caffeine and that blasted decommissioned air conditioner.

"And what did he say?"

"That you've fallen behind rent. After having a spotty payment schedule to begin with."

"Gideon, what's going on," Lizzy finally said. "Are we going under, or what?"

"No, it's not like that?"

"Well, then, are you embezzling?" Reggie asked.

A flash of angry heat rose to my cheeks. "No," I said firmly, insulted he even went there. "It's not like that, either."

"Then what the hell is it like, Gideon?" he asked, voice

rising in a way I usually appreciated, because it meant he was closing the deal in the courtroom.

Now...not so much.

I stood, darting for a black mini fridge left over from college, weighed down by another pile of folders a foot or two high. Buying time but also seeking relief.

I crouched and opened the door, relief flooding me with visions of hydrated saturation dancing in my head.

A single Dasani.

I grabbed it and twisted off the top, bringing it to my lips.

Only to realize the other two were probably equally as thirsty. I hesitated, glancing their way, but they both nodded for me to have at it.

A twinge of guilt wound its way through me, but not enough to stay my hand. I took it back to my desk, gulping back the blessed water before slumping back in my chair.

"So?" Reggie said, mouth open now and sweat dribbling down the side of his clean-shaven head he seemed to be ignoring. Was clearly more focused on me and my answers, or lack of them, than his own discomfort.

And for good reason.

I'd gone silent because the man was exposing something I'd long known about, but was too ashamed to admit.

I went with: "I've just fallen behind paying, that's all." It was the truth. I had.

"Fallen behind?" Reggie said, sounding exasperated.

"Three, going on four months worth?" Lizzy added.

"And several times over?"

I was getting hot under the collar, now. And not from the blasted air conditioner being taken out of commission.

"There's been a cash flow issue on and off all year."

Reggie twisted up his face in confusion. "All year?"

"And when that blasted virus hit this spring, things became more precarious."

"But that can't be all of it," Lizze said, "because we've been getting paid just fine. And there have been some big settlements lately as work has picked back up."

Work had picked up. Which was part of the problem, trying to keep my head above water with some new clients and big cases, on top of getting our names out there to drum up new business, a hamster wheel or rat race or pick your analogy that was running me ragged.

"Hello, Gideon?" Reggie asked, voice laced with annoyance.

I startled and took another swig of water, then snapped back: "What?"

He looked at Lizzy. "I said, what's the deal then, if we're getting paid but you can't make rent?"

"Like I said, cash flow."

"But—"

"I'm bad at administration. So sue me!"

"But that's so unlike you, Gideon," Lizzy said. "You're a powerhouse. That's why we came to work for you."

"Yeah, Gideon, what's happened," Reggie added. "What's the root of it, then?"

"The root? I can't do it all, Reggie!" I finally yelled, exploding under the weight of the interrogation and suffocation of the mid-morning heat. "That's the root if it, then!"

I instantly regretted my outburst but didn't know what to do. So I threw back the rest of my Dasani.

"Hey, Gideon," Lizzy said, scooching to the edge of her seat, "no one is asking you to!"

"Yeah, my man," Reggie said, voice low and buttery and apologetic. "That's why we're here. To help."

I took a breath and sighed, leaning back in my chair.

"I'm sorry. Sorry for the outburst. And thanks for the support. I'll do better next time."

"Do better?" Lizzy said.

"I'll catch up on the payments, sending out what we owe. I'll set a schedule and get back on track. Don't worry. I've got this."

Lizzy smiled and looked down at her lap, then back at me. "But that's the thing, Gideon. You don't."

I was stunned. Too stunned for words.

"Other things have been falling through the cracks."

"Such as?" I said quickly, coming to my defense and regretting it.

She took a breath. "Such as...follow-up calls to new clients not happening, follow-up with long-time clients not happening. Some of the—"

"Alright, I get it."

Then she looked at Reggie and nodded. She nodded back, and he leaned forward.

"And, well, that's part of what we want to talk about," Reggie said, shifting in his seat but clearly getting ready to go for the kill.

And I was the prey.

"Oh, yeah?" I said, staring at the ceiling. "What's that?"

He didn't even wait a beat. "We want equity."

Just like that. That was their demand. To own a piece of what I had built.

I was stunned. Too stunned for words, for a second time. Literally. I couldn't get anything out.

"Partners?" was the only thing I could manage.

"Not in equal measure," Lizzy added, shifting back into her seat and pushing back a stray lock of hair. "But something. We want skin in the game. And we want to help. Help build the practice, help you manage it all."

I scoffed. "Help? You want to own the game, you mean?"

She went silent. So did Reggie.

Traffic humming outside on Main Street was the only soundtrack for the tragedy. Or comedy, depending how you looked at it.

"It's like the book of Ecclesiastes says, Gideon," Reggie said, finally breaking the silence.

"Please don't quote scripture to me right now, Reggie..." I moaned, taking a swig of coffee to dull a pain beginning to needled the middle of my forehead.

"Naw, man, you need to hear this. It's not preachy scripture, just some wisdom my mama would remind me of from time to time. Chapter 4 says: *'Two are better than one, because they have a good reward for their toil. For if they fall, one will lift up the other; but woe to one who is alone and falls and does not have another to help. Again, if two lie together, they keep warm; but how can one keep warm alone? And though one might prevail against another, two will withstand one. A threefold cord is not quickly broken.'*"

He paused glancing at Lizzy, who continued: "That's what this is about, Gideon. Building this unbreakable cord, the three of us. In this fight for justice, not only for all our sakes, but for our clients."

She did have a point. As much as I didn't like the idea about giving up control, about no longer going it alone, managing it all had become a burden. The oppressive heat was Exhibit A on that one.

I went to respond when something caught my eye across the room, anchored to a wall struggling under the weight of sagging bookshelves.

A framed one dollar bill.

The first buck I'd made at my practice, before Reggie and Lizzy had joined as associates.

There'd been a lot of sweat and sleepless nights and even some tears since that first buck I'd been paid. I'd lost some cases, won a whole heck of a lot more. Clients had walked out and left me high and dry, others we'd picked up on retainer. Immigrants and their jobs and families had been protected. Wrongfully accused murderers had been spared life sentences—gotten a few questionable ones off on technicalities, too, but it was in the interest of upholding and preserving our civil liberties. Then there were the settlements and judgments we'd gotten from hospitals and corporations for negligent disregard and wrongful termination.

The list went on. All thanks to that dollar bill sitting behind that dusty glass in that cheap bronze frame.

But then it hit me. Because that wasn't the truth of it. The full truth, anyway.

Two are better than one, because they have a good reward for their toil...

All that toil, all those other dollar bills since that first one were because of the pair sitting across from me. Problem was, I hadn't let them have a share in the praise and honor of it all.

A strand of three cords, huh?

One end of my mouth curled upward, something melting inside at the thought. Maybe it was my hard heart or thick head from being confronted and getting exposed. Probably that, but it was more. Less about embarrassment from exposure, more about possibilities from partnership.

I stood, shirt sticking to my back now and feeling like I was about to pass out. I walked toward the door then motioned for my associates—for my *partners*.

"Let's take a walk."

The cooler air hit me like a welcomed hug, not as stifling as my office but the air still warm and stale and hanging with a pause. I took in a breath, old carpet and paint combined with roasted coffee and stacks of photo-copied paper all combining to remind me what this was for. More than the smells and feel of the place was what I saw: two desks piled high with cases, surrounded by more boxes and file cabinets filled with more cases—wins and losses, but mostly wins—the whole place manned by two co-laborers fighting for justice with everything they had.

What more could I ask for?

What more could *Mill Creek Junction* ask for?

"See this place?" I said, motioning around the room with both hands. "After law school, I came back to the Junc-tion on a whim thanks to my old man suggesting I set out on my own and chart my own course and see what happened. Well, this is what happened. But not thanks to me."

I turned toward the pair still standing behind me at my door. "Thanks to you two. So, yeah, you more than deserve an equity stake." Then I smiled. "You both deserve to make partner, as little as that might mean in this modest practice."

There was silence, as if Reggie and Lizzy hadn't heard me right.

Then they also broke out in smiles, their mouths widening into toothy grins of thanksgiving, a cheer rising from them both before they reached out with an embrace.

My throat grew tight with a surprising rise of emotion. And I laughed at the display, especially since we were all soaking with sweat now. But it didn't matter. We were part-ners, or would be soon enough once we completed the paperwork. But more than that, we were family—a word that hadn't always sat right with me as an adopted child, left at a firehouse and raised by two black parents who gave me the world but had still carried baggage, my soul feeling incomplete in some way from my personal history.

That moment reminded me that I had all the family I'd ever need with the people in my life.

"So what do we call ourselves?" Reggie asked, leaning back and getting down to business. Always one to cut the bull and get to it, which is why I liked him so much.

"You mean which order should our names go in, right?" I said, one end of my mouth curling upward.

"Obviously by level of seniority," Lizzy quickly offered, "with Gideon's name at the front."

"Makes sense," Reggie said.

"So *O'Donnell, Seward, and Wilson,* then?"

He took a beat, then smiled and nodded. "I like the sound of that."

"Me, too!" Lizzy said, breaking out in another grin.

"Taking on that knucklehead Prosecuting Attorney Dean Lawlor and whoever else wants a piece of our justice! The three of us together."

I nodded and smiled myself. "Yes. Together."

As much as I hated to admit it, going it alone for so much of my life, that word was music to my ears. Last thing I thought would happen turning forty earlier in the year. But Reggie's wisdom, or I guess the Bible's, sounded pretty solid.

A threefold cord is not quickly broken.

The three of us locked arm-in-arm will be unbreakable.

No, *Unstoppable.*

Mill Creek Junction won't know what hit them.

STORY 3

NEVER IN A MILLION YEARS

NEVER IN A MILLION YEARS.

That's what I've told friends from around town and from back East when they've asked how I ended up at Mill Creek Junction Baptist.

Never in a million years did I think I'd be pastoring, let alone attending, a church the likes of Mill Creek Junction Baptist. Forming a relationship with this small town in this pastoral sort of way.

On some level it made sense, since I was born and raised in the tradition on the other side of Grand Rapids in Coopersville, the armpit of Michigan, that's for sure. Not Coopersville Baptist, mind you. Them good folk, with their tater tot casseroles and coffee tasting of cardboard left out in the sun too long and three-man band praise music still stuck in the 90s. All three of which fit Mill Creek Junction Baptist to a T.

Maybe that's what led me to apply in the first place. Not that I had many prospects after graduating Grand River Theological Seminary, or anything. It's not like preaching is a booming trade. But I guess what they say is right: familiarity breeds contentment. Or is it contempt. Now that I think about it, I'm not quite sure. Either way, there I was, walking out of my first week serving alongside Reiner Alden, or the Rev as he's affectionately known around the Junction.

And I needed a drink.

Thankfully, the Rev was cool with my pastime, which was unexpected. Baptists generally still thought alcohol was the result of man's fall from grace. As if the scientific properties of fermentation suddenly spontaneously arose after Mama Eve and Papa Adam ate the forbidden fruit and rebelled against God, dragging all of our sorry backsides down into the dumps of chaos and sin and death.

Me, and thankfully the Rev—though I'm not sure the rest of the congregation was in on his theological position—we were both under the assumption that wine and beer and strong spirits were part of God's good creation. That God the Father, creator of heaven and earth, built into the created order the process and properties for his creatures to enjoy the effects of fermented grapes and fermented hops and fermented barley. After all, there were plenty of places in the Holy Scriptures where the good Lord above encouraged his people to enjoy the fruits of such creative labor. In fact, the consummation of all things when the good Lord himself returns at the end of the age is often compared to a banquet where strong wine is served. So as far as we were concerned, alcohol was a gift from God's very good creation that was meant to be enjoyed. In moderation, of course.

And thank God the Father for that! Because my mouth was watering for some of the fruits of his creative order.

But given, the last time I'd shown up at Max's Place, I wasn't so sure I wanted a round two. Yet it was the only joint in town. So off I went, heading down the halls of the new edition still smelling of new paint and plaster, locking my door and stuffing the shiny silver key in my pocket.

"Have a good weekend, Peter Daniel Young!" Rev Alden said, popping his head out the door.

I smiled and chuckled. "Peter's fine, Mr. Alden."

"And Reinier is fine for me, Petey. That is what your friends call you, right?"

"My parents, actually. But sometimes my girlfriend, too."

"Lexy, right?"

"That's right. I think she's going to make the service next week. She's been eager to meet the man who's been stealing all my time this first week."

He frowned, rubbing the back of his neck. "Yeah, sorry about that, Peter."

"No, it's no problem at all," I said, putting up a hand. "She's just happy I got a job outside her coffee shop." We shared a laugh.

I continued, "Seriously, though, she's happy for me. I'm happy for me! Thanks for the week. For the job."

Alden smiled and nodded. "No, Peter. Thank you. We're blessed to have you. And so am I. But seriously, though, get out of here! I've taken enough of your time this week. Go do something fun!"

"Yes, sir!"

I gave a half salute and headed out onto Main Street, the summer sun beginning to hang a bit lower now that August had arrived. Which made me both happy and sad. Sad that the laid back pace of summer was drawing to a close, but happy that meant my favorite season was just around the corner.

Fall!

And judging by the large oaks and maples and

sycamores edging Main Street and all the other streets across the Junction, I'd be in for a real treat with all their multi-colored glow. But for now, I was enjoying the dry low-80s that had descended on West Michigan on my walk over to Max's Place, the smell of grills grilling and the sound of laughter filtering in from the surrounding twentieth-century bungalows and craftsman homes arrayed in neat rows across blocks of neighborhoods that screamed quintessential small-town Americana.

Which was funny, because I'd never pictured myself living in quintessential small-town Americana. Not after fleeing West Michigan after going to college in quintessential small-town Americana in Virginia for Washington, DC, after having been raised in quintessential small-town Americana Coopersville, Michigan. Been there, done that, got the beer koozie to prove it!

Yet there I was, waving to Sherif Roller, who seemed like a nice fella, though probably misunderstood. Then passing Millie's on Main, the scent of her meat loaf special hovering just outside the door with a line trailing it a block. And sighting Old Man Nugent's barber joint, which reminded me I was in desperate need of a haircut. Which also meant Max's Place was nearing.

There was a line, which I found amusing. Aside from two other chain restaurants on the outskirts of town, Max's Place was about the closest thing you'd get to a good meal and drink. But I sensed the popularity was more than that. My last visit with the Rev was where I'd met the owner, Max Blade himself. He was a bit of a character, but a solid character. A guy's guy who meant well, who made you feel at ease and at home. A real stand-up fella who you'd want to sit down and have a beer with, even if he did own the joint. People were lining up to see

Max as much as they were lining up to get into Max's Place.

Soon enough, I was at the front door, and I was staring the man himself straight in the face. He did a double take until he recognized me. Surprisingly, his serious, all-business face softened into a full-on grin, and he was ushering me inside.

"Preacherman!" he said, as he ushered me inside. "Didn't expect to see you so soon after the hell we put you through a few weeks ago."

Some band was doing a sound check on a platform at the back, the cacophony of the full house of patrons drowning out most of it.

"Yeah, well, figured I'd kick back after my first week on the job."

He stopped suddenly, a sea of bodies and faces I still didn't recognize surrounding us in the middle of the bar.

"Your first week on the job?" he asked, his mouth going slack and eyes bugging out. "So, what, you taking over for the Rev? He retiring or something?"

There was something to his tone that surprised me. A reverence combined with a disappointment, as if he was super bummed his best friend wouldn't be around again for the next school year.

I said, "I think it's going to be a while until the man retires, if that's what you're worried about."

His face slackened and he nodded, as if in relief. "Good, well, let's get you something to eat. And a drink! On the house." He ushered me up to the bar.

"That's not necessary."

"No, man, I insist! A man survives his first week of work. And at a church, no less, and he deserves a free meal and a free round. Next one's on you though," he said with a wink, seating me at the same bar chair I'd sat at a few weeks ago when I thought I'd offended the whole lot of them. Guess I hadn't if the guy was giving me the red carpet treatment. Maybe that meant I could have a nice night of peace and quiet.

Max went around back and asked, "What do you want, preacherman?"

I picked up the menu and started flipping through the thing. "How about a burger and a beer?"

"Burger and a beer. We can do that! How you like your meat?"

"Medium rare, if they still let you do that nowadays."

He grinned. "My kind of guy. Medium rare it is!" He shouted to the back my order, adding a stack of sweet potato fries on the side. "And IPAs were your thing, if I remembered correctly. And Grey Goose, although I'd imagine it's a little early for that."

I chuckled. "Probably. And yeah, an IPA would be great."

"Bell's Two Hearted, coming up!"

I thanked him and took in the lay of the land, with all the people and conversations and the pace of the place.

Mayor Goodall was hamming it up with a table across the room, working it like the politician he was. Which made sense, given it was an election year. His wife Millie rolled her eyes before grinning, shaking a finger before rolling her eyes again, eliciting a round of laughs at something.

Sheriff Roller had just shown up, head shiny beneath the lights over head, and was pouring himself a drink from a half-drained pitcher a table over, similarly all big-toothed and full-on belly laugh. Then he poured one for Old Man Nugent, as I understood his name, the town barber. Nice guy who gave a decent haircut for a good price.

Ken and Barbara sat together across the room, enjoying a moment alone after adding a newborn to their family a few weeks back. Then there was Dean Lawlor, commanding another table of his prosecuting attorneys,. One of those prosecutors, Annabelle Kirkland, was looking bored and checking her watch and glancing at another table across the way at Gideon O'Donnell, who was commanding his own table of his legal associates, Reggie and Lizzy, and a few other lawyers from around town. Another table of farmers and farmhands were nursing their own pitchers and chawing it up over baskets of fries and burgers, with Fred Myers adding his two cents, the local grocer.

The whole thing made me smile, a cross section of town all gathered together under one roof, with Max Blade the ringleader of the circus. Had to admit, it was nice. A nice town of nice people, dealing with their fair share of issues, but getting by and getting along.

Never in a million years.

"Here you go, partner," Max said, setting down my beer with his cook Burt behind him, coming around to set down a plate with my burger and fries. Then he sat down next to me and huffed a tired sigh.

"That was fast," I said, nodding at Burt, who was wiping his bald black head with a towel.

"You mind if I join you for a spell?" he asked.

I swallowed back a hoppy swig of Bells. "Not a bit. Just don't let the beef burn or I'd imagine Max would have your hide."

Burt chuckled. "Don't you know it."

"I wouldn't have your hide!" Max said. "I'd just have your paycheck."

He threw his sweaty towel at the guy, who ducked.

"Hey, honey," someone said, coming up from behind

with a sort of drawl I'd expected from someone back East. "This seat taken?"

It was Sheila, one of Max's servers. A rail-thin lady with tanned, wrinkled skin who looked a tad frazzled. Apparently, it was break time for Max's top lieutenants, and during my dinner break. But I didn't mind. Would give me a chance to get to know a few of the fixtures of the Junction. Maybe even deepen my relationships with these fine Junction folk.

My mouth was full with my first burger bite, so I motioned for her to sit. She'd already commandeered the stool but smiled and thanked me anyway.

"Burger alright for your likin'?" Max asked, now leaning over the bar toward me and hovering as well.

I swallowed and cleared my throat with a swig of beer. "It's perfect. Like, perfect!"

And I wasn't lying! The perfect amount of pink, moist and juicy, with crisp lettuce and a fresh tomato, slathered in brown mustard and catsup, rubbed with some sort of concoction tasting of paprika and coffee and pepper.

I held it up and eyed it. "This rubbed with some sort of special spice or something?"

Burt chuckled. "You could say that. Something I dreamed up one day. You takin' to it alright?"

"Taking to it? I might hold you hostage until you give up your secret, it's so good!" We shared a laugh.

"So, preacherman..." Max said, taking the washcloth to the bar top, "has preaching always been your specialty?"

I smiled at the name that now seemed to be my nickname. I guess I could be annoyed, taking it as a slight or something. But I chose to embrace it as a term of endearment. Seemed to be Max's way.

I swallowed again and threw back another swig of beer.

"Not always. Used to work on Capital Hill. For the Speaker of the House, actually, before getting into the ministry gig."

Max frowned. "Politics and religion, huh?"

"Betcha you real popular at dinner parties, ain't'cha?" Burt said with a chuckle.

I smiled. "Which is why I don't get out much."

"Don't pay them no mind, honey," Sheila said.

"I ain't got much time for religion, myself," Burt said, slouching back in his seat, huffing out a tired breath, as if the weight of the world were on his shoulders.

I wondered about the man—his life, his story. Early 60s, no wedding band that I could see. And a black man in the Junction was a tough thing. Not so much now, but for sure growing up.

"Not that I ain't a believer or nothing," he quickly added. "I was raised right proper in the church. Mill Creek Baptist, in fact. Just sorta faded away. Gave up on Christianity meaning anything in the day-to-day grind, you get what I'm sayin'?"

I nodded. "Totally understand."

Then Max himself leaned forward. "What I want to know is if you've always bought into the whole Christian thing."

"Oh, come on, Max," Sheila said. "Let the poor kid eat in peace."

Direct and to the point. Didn't expect anything less from the guy, from what I had seen. Which was fine by me.

"Naw, it's alright," I said, throwing back another swig of beer. "I don't mind talking about my faith." I took a breath. Time to get personal. Felt right. And, why not? The mood seemed right. Again: maybe forge some deeper bonds.

"Truth is, I actually understand very well this pull to sort of give up on Christianity. As you said, Burt."

Burt crossed his arm and nodded, growing silent.

"Really?" Max said, brow raised with surprise. "You're, like, a pastorman. A defender and protector of the Christian faith, or something."

I chuckled. "Well, before I was a pastorman I was a regular Joe Blow trying to make sense of faith, life, and everything in between."

"Sort of like Spiderman before he got bit by that alien spider?"

"Something like that."

"Don't listen to these yokels," Sheila said. Then she pointed at Max, adding: "Especially this one."

Max frowned. "What, me?"

"Go on, then," Burt said, nodding with arms still folded. "What's your own journey with the Church?"

I shifted in my seat then drained my beer. Max promptly picked it up and began pulling me a refile. "This one ain't on the house."

"Then it's on me, then," Burt said.

I went to object but nodded my thanks.

"In my mid-twenties," I started, "I followed the same path of disillusionment with the Church many have. In response to the skepticism and multiple religions and problems in the Church I've had deep doubts, deep questions about faith and life."

"Like what?" Sheila asked, leaning in now as well.

I cleared my throat again, a cold wave of panic washing over me as I got even more personal about my faith. Wondered what Alden, or the Rev as he was known in these parts, would think about my honesty. But as I looked at Max, who was fixing me with serious, searching eyes, and nodding, as if cheering me onward, a dose of courage to share my own experience with Christianity flooded my veins.

So I did.

"I've wondered," I started before adding: "I *still* wonder sometimes, even though I'm an ordained pastor, that if God is so good, why is life so bad? I've wondered if the God of the Bible is really the only God—is Jesus the only way to the Father. I've wondered what on earth Jesus and his life means for me and my life, like right now, before death. I've wondered how big and wide and vast is the love of God, and what that means for everyone from the beginning of time to the end of time."

"Those are some deep questions, preacherman," Max said.

"Don't I know it!" I chuckled, the others joining in. "That's not even the half of it!"

"What's the other half of it then?" Burt asked, face fallen a bit and head cocked with his own level of interest.

"The other half," I went on, "is that in my darkest days I've wondered if all of this Christian faith and Church stuff is just a sham. Sort of like the Wizard of Oz, just a bunch of people behind a curtain."

The cook leaned back and folded her arms. "That's deep."

"And ballsy for sharing," Max said, stiffening and folding his arms himself. "Gotta give you that one. You know, seen as how you're a preacherman and all."

I smiled and finished my beer. "Just don't let it get out, alright?"

"Dontcha worry," Burt said, nodding. "Your secret's safe with us. Because I'm pretty sure if it got out you're entertainin' doubts about the faith, the Junction wayward would have a field day!"

Max snorted a laugh. "Yeah, like the Pope doubting apostolic succession!"

"Hold, on," Sheila said, putting up a hand. "If I hear Peter right, he said he had *wondered*. Past tense."

I nodded. "That's right. It's more that I've been there. I get it. Not that the spectre of my doubt doesn't visit from time to time. And, if we're honest, maybe you've had some similar questions. Maybe you *still* have some similar questions—about faith, about life, about the Church."

All three nodded, as if understanding completely.

I chuckled before widening into a grin. "Anyone else want to share their own deepest, darkest struggles with the Christian faith?"

They echoed my chuckle, laughing with recognition at the truth of their own struggles, but shaking their heads and growing silent.

"Didn't think so," I said, eliciting another round of laughs.

"I will ask one more question, though" Max said.

Sheila stood and complained, "I think we've done enough damage for one night, fellas. Wasted the poor kid's private dinner pestering him with questions."

I said, "No, it's alright. Go ahead, Max. But make it another IPA."

He smiled and grabbed my drink and started pulling another from the tap. Finishing, he set down the glass and asked, "What changed?"

"And what keeps you on the straight and narrow, so to speak?" Burt asked.

I sat forward with interest, enjoying the back and forth now and reminded me of my work at Georgetown University back in DC, sitting with college students wrestling with their faith.

"There's pretty much one thing that's kept me on the straight and narrow, Burt, as you said. The same thing that changed it for me those years ago."

"Oh, yeah, preacherman?" Max asked, leaning against the bar top again. Then, with an almost interested whisper barely audible above the din of the crowd: "What's that?"

I waited a beat, then said, "The resurrection."

"The what?" Sheila asked, having sat down again.

Max answered, "He's speaking about the Christian doctrine that Jesus came back to life all zombie like."

I laughed. "Not a zombie. Jesus isn't un-dead, he defeated death! Was raised from the dead by God the Father. That singular event drove the disciples to go to the mat for their belief that through Jesus' death and resurrection, God was rescuing the world and putting it back together again. It was the consistent, core, foundational belief of the early church and earliest disciples. I figured, why die for a lie? But there was something else that drove it home for me. Evidence I couldn't shake, even in my darkest moments."

I paused, taking a breath and taking another swig, letting the silence pique their interest.

When too much time ticked by, Max raised his hands and said, "And? Come on, preacherman, don't leave us hanging!"

I set down my drink. "And, it was the Shroud of Turin."

"The shroud-o-what?" Burt asked, face wrinkled up with confusion.

"It's the purported burial cloth of Jesus. It's this, almost sheet-like-thing with this image of a man imprinted on the cloth, on front and back sitting side-by-side: underneath his closed eyes is a mustache and beard, and long hair falling beyond his shoulders to the center of his back; his arms are crossed, one hand over the other, and engraved with several white markings; hundreds more of the same white etchings are on the man's back and chest, crisscrossing each other at jagged right angles; similar white zig-zags mark the crown of his head and seems to be dripping down his forehead; the same white lacerations mark both sides of his legs. It's really crazy, and I discovered the depth of it through this professor from Princeton, this guy named Silas Grey."

"Never heard of him," Max said.

"Who's he?" Sheila asked. "And what's this shroud business?"

"Guy no longer works there, but ever since watching an episode of *Unsolved Mysteries* as a boy that chronicled the history and mystery of the Shroud, I have been fascinated with the fourteen-by-nine foot ancient Church relic."

Max stared off and mumbled, "*Unsolved Mysteries...* Now that you mention it, the Shroud of Turin, or whatever, sounds vaguely familiar."

"It's a really fascinating relic. But as a thoroughly Protestant Christian who later became a thoroughly Evangelical pastor, I probably shouldn't have held onto this fascination. After all, our kind tends not to put much stock in such things for grounding our faith. And yet a verse from the Book of Acts has always needled away at my mind and faith."

"Aww, here we go," he said. "Preacherman gettin' his preach on!"

I put up a hand. "No, not that. Just listen. Acts 1:3 says: *'After his suffering he presented himself alive to them [the apostles] by many convincing proofs, appearing to them during forty days and speaking about the kingdom of God.'* Think about that: Jesus Christ, the Son of God, bodily raised from the dead to new life, offered his followers many more *'infallible proofs'* that he was in fact alive! Another version says that Jesus *'gave many convincing proofs that he was alive,'* as if the disciples needed more evidence that Jesus rose from the dead than the fact he was standing in front of them with nail-scarred hands and a gaping wound in his side."

"So what of it?" Burt asked.

"So, I've wondered, what if the Shroud was one of those convincing proofs? And why not? Especially given the mountain of evidence that seems to point toward its authenticity. And that evidence is what this story is built upon, that the Shroud is real and that it preserves the memory of this vital aspect of the vintage Christian faith: the resurrection of Jesus Christ, which is proof positive that his sacrifice for the sins of the world worked and that his gift of new life is genuine."

"And what is that evidence?" Max asked, one brow raised with skepticism and the other seeming like it was holding on to interest.

I took a swig and checked the time. This was getting long, but they seemed to be interested, so I kept going.

"You've got the faint imprint visible on the linen, which is that of a real corpse in rigor mortis. In fact, the image is of a crucified victim. The anatomical realism of the image was so precise that separation of serum and cellular mass was evident in many of the blood stains. This is an important characteristic of dried blood. Which means there is real, actual dried human blood embedded in the cloth."

Sheila shuddered. "Creepy."

I smiled, then continued, "There is swelling around the eyes, the natural reaction to bruising from a beating. The New Testament claims Jesus was severely beaten before his crucifixion. Rigor mortis is also evident with the enlarged chest and distended feet, classic marks of an actual crucifixion. Which means the man in that burial linen was mutilated in exactly the same manner that the New Testament says Jesus of Nazareth was beaten, whipped, and executed by means of crucifixion."

"And this sheet of yours confirms that?" Burt asked, brows raised with surprise.

"That's right. But one of the more fascinating aspects of the Shroud is that it is a negative image, not a positive one. That technology was not even understood until the nineteenth century with the invention of the camera when photography became a modern reality. Which blows holes in the oft purported theory that the Shroud is merely a Medieval forgery that was stained or pained. It would be a thousand years until such ideas as negative images were understood, which no Medieval artist could have painted!"

"That's crazy talk!" Max said.

"You're telling me, pal! What's even crazier is the positive image taken from the negative one left on the Shroud shows in detail many of the historic markers that connect to the Gospel accounts of Jesus' death. "

"Like what, honey?" Sheila asked, seemingly hanging on every word now.

"Well, you have the scourging marks from a Roman flagrum on the arms, legs, and back. Lacerations around the head from the crown of thorns. His shoulder appears to be dislocated, probably from carrying his cross beam and falling. All consistent with the eyewitness accounts recorded in the Gospels."

I was on a roll and kept going, getting to the best evidence of all.

"The image of the man, with all of his facial features and hair and wounds, is absolutely unique. Nothing like it in all the world. Totally inexplicable. And given there are no stains indicating decomposition on the linen itself, we know that whatever body was in the Shroud left before the decomposition process began. Just as the Gospel writers testify about Jesus' resurrection from the dead on the third day. The odds against this image being someone other than Jesus are astronomical. 225...billion to 1, according to Paul de Gail, a French Jesuit priest and engineer. Which means it is not unreasonable to conclude that the man in the Shroud is indeed the historical person we know of as Jesus of Nazareth, around whom—his life, death, and resurrection—the Christian faith was launched and built."

I paused looking off, taking another breath and another swig, one end curling with wonderment at what I believed to be true about what God had preserved for the world as proof of Jesus' resurrection. "That the man imprinted on the Shroud is that of Jesus of Nazareth doesn't in and of itself prove or disprove that Jesus came back to life and rose from the dead. But there are strong indications that, at the very least, something extraordinary and very unusual occurred in the cloth. And so that's why I continue to believe. On top of what the Bible testifies to."

The table settled into a sort of holy silence, as if all at once contemplating and agreeing with my assessment.

"Never in a million years would something like resurrecting a man from the dead be possible. Yet the witness of twentysomethings who went to the mat for their faith confirms this, the science of the relic seems to confirm it, and the truth of Jesus' resurrection has been confirmed in my own life as well as billions of others across the millennia."

"Can't say I believe with you, preacherman," Max finally said. "But you know what?"

One end of my mouth curled upward with curiosity. "What's that?"

He grabbed a glass and started pulling another drink. "I appreciate you sharing just the same. Not just what you believe, but that you've doubted some. Does my heart right good. So I'll drink to that!"

Burt made a motion toward Max as he finished with a glass half full. "So will I. Why don't you give me one of those."

"And me!" Sheila said.

Max scoffed. "You're both still on the job, for Pete's sake!"

Burt scoffed back. "And you ain't?"

"I own the joint!"

Now Burt and Sheila were complaining loudly, threatening to walk off the job and leave him high and dry."

"Alright, calm yer yappers, would ya?" Max said, dopping in a few sips worth into two glasses for the pair. He handed them off and added: "And don't you even think about complaining about the paltry sum inside."

"Paltry?" Sheila said, raising a brow.

Burt added, "A right big word for someone so—"

"I'm warning you..." Max complained.

Sheila shut her mouth and stifled a giggle.

"Yes, Mista Masta," Burt said, doing the same.

Max rolled his eyes and raised his glass. "To Peter."

I raised mine. "To the resurrection."

He chuckled then said "Touché" before throwing back half the glass.

So did Burt and Sheila, as did I—almost disbelieving I was sitting in a no-name bar in a no-name town sharing a bit of my spiritual journey with three fine folks who were more than interested in what I had to say. And about the Christian belief in the resurrection, no less!

Where my relationship with this town, its people, would go—the good Lord only knew!

Yet there I was, drinking beer with the people who he had put in my path. People I would minister to in the coming years. People I would marry and bury. People who had deep spiritual questions about faith, life, and everything in between.

Never in a million years, indeed.

STORY 4

A NIGHT ON THE COUNTRYSIDE

"ALRIGHT, Burt, Sheila, I'm peacing out for the night," I said, the night still young but the day still old, if you get my drift.

"We've got it covered, Max!" Sheila said.

Burt nodded. "Yeah, boss, it's all good. Go and have yourself a night of peace and quiet."

I took a step toward the door, then spun around. "Are you sure? I mean, I could cancel on the boys and hold down fort—"

"Go on, git," Sheila said, smacking me on my shoulder and shooin' me outta my own joint now with her hands like they were a pair of flippers.

"Alright, alright!" I said, holding up my paws in defense and hightailing it outta there just as a rock number from way back started up at the stage in the back. "Just don't burn the place—"

Now she came at me with a broom, and that's when I got out of Dodge.

Or Max's Place, which was really my place. The best dang bar in Mill Creek Junction, if I don't say so myself.

Actually, the only dang bar in the Junction, thanks to a zoning ordinance from way back in Prohibition that my grandpappy had cleared by the hair of his chinny chin chin. But that's another story.

One that mattered not a lick, for tonight was my first night off since we opened the place back up after our Dear Leader let us start congregatin' on the other side of that dang virus. And what a night it was.

The sun had set an hour ago, the fallout setting the horizon on fire in a blaze of orange and red glory. The street lamps lining Main Street flickered to life, casting a yellow glow across the center street of the town awash with a weird fog rollin' on in. A town I'd always complained about and vowed to leave but never did anything about. And glad I didn't.

Mill Creek was home, my home. It was me and I was it. I mean, no way on God's green Earth would the Junction be the Junction without Max's Place. That'd be like Thelma without Louise. Bonnie without Clyde. Batman without Robin, for Pete's sake!

Oh, yes, two peas in a pod, we were. And one of us was taking the night off. Spendin' it with a pair of cool cats who were in for a night of fun. Didn't know what I had in store for 'em yet, but oo-wee!

It was gonna be a good night, a night out on the country-side. The best nights ever!

"There he is. The man of the hour." Gideon O'Donnell was leaning against my gold Plymouth Breeze.

The Golden Nugget, I called her. Been with me for a pair of decades and never let me down. Although, couldn't say the same for Daimler Chrysler sending their ol' Plymouth brand out to pasture way back when. No matter. The beast had just crested two-hundo-thousand miles and was still goin' strong! Granted, nearly every part had been replaced a time or three the past pair of decades. About the only thing left untouched was the engine and plush beige cabin. Lotta firsts in that car, yessiree.

In fact, we were fixin' to add another that night. Unbeknownst to the fellas.

"Yeah, the man, the myth, the legend. Max Blade himself." Johnny Pope stepped out from the shadows of Old Man Nugent's barbershop joint bearing the goods. A pair of Pabst Blue Ribbon twelve packs. Just what the doc ordered, and the night demanded.

Given what I had in store.

I disengaged the remote security, the *chirp, chirp* echoing down Main.

Gideon stepped off from the car, still wearing his lawyerly getup, and stared back at it as I strolled up. "Really, Max? You've got that thing armed?"

"And dangerous. Never can be too careful when a vintage car is on the line, even in the Junction."

The man laughed. "Vintage?"

I scrunched up my brow. "Yeah. Vintage. You feel what I'm talkin' 'bout, dontcha, JP?"

Johnny Pope seemed to be stiflin' a smile but nodded. "Yeah, I feel ya, parter. Let's roll in this *vintage* getup of yours."

I grinned. "Music to my ears. I see you brought your half of the goods."

He raised the pair of PBR twelve packs. "That I did."

"And you, partner?" I said, looking at Gideon.

He held up a box of Ritz Crackers in one hand and a package of salami and hard cheese from Meyer's General in the other. "That I did. But I gotta say, what the heck are you expecting us to do with this?"

I went around to the driver's side door and unlocked the Golden Nugget, all four doors. "Eat it, what else? Between that and the PBR, we'll be set for the night. Fo sho!"

"Whatever you say..." he mumbled.

I slid inside and told the other cool cats to do the same, then roared the Breeze to life. When everyone was buckled in nice and tight, Gideon riding shotgun and JP in the middle rear, I threw her in *Drive* and eased her onto Main. Soon we were cruisin' east outta downtown Mill Creek on toward destiny.

Where was anyone's guess.

Except for mine.

I rolled my window down, the night wind blowing my golden mane, then I popped in a CD mixtape I'd made for the trip and cranked the volume, the angsty electrics and *rat-a-tat-tats* of the snare opening up "Born to Be Wild." Soon we were followin' Steppenwolf's advice: our motor was runnin' smooth as a baby's bottom, we were headin' for a county road, and crusin' toward adventure.

Come what may!

"Lovely taste in music," Gideon moaned, rolling down his own window and hanging his arm out.

"How about you loosen up that getup of yours," I said.

He frowned and looked down at the noose still clinging to his neck. "What's wrong with it?"

"You're zipped up tighter than a nun in that thing! With the tucked-in shirt and tie cinched like a noose 'round that skinny neck of yours. No wonder you're wound up tighter than a—"

"I ain't wound up tighter than anything!" he complained, pulling out that tie of his and throwing it in my face.

"Hey, watch it!" I veered in the other lane for dramatic

effect. When an eighteen-wheeler belched a wicked warning and flashed its peepers at us.

Which sent the boys a'screamin' like a bunch of school girls! Laughed so hard I thought I was gonna pee my pants.

"Don't worry, fellas! Max Blade's got it all under control!"

Now Johnny Pope smacked me upside the head. I jerked the wheel just a pinch, but that set 'em off again so I apologized and sped farther out past the Junction into the open road that was Mill Creek's eastern flank.

"What's with this fog, anyhow?" he asked.

"Radiation fog," I said, straightening out my arm and high-fiving the air rushing past.

Gideon looked at me. "Come again?"

"You know. Due to the cooling of the earth's surface at night. Given how hot it was right before that cooling storm came in, the earth normally radiates off heat absorbed from the Sun's light during the day. As the warm air rises, the air near the earth's surface becomes cooler, especially after that wicked front rolled up in here, dragging in that cooler air of Lake Michigan into the inner parts of the state and mixin' with the heated land."

"A regular Bill Nye the Science Guy aren't ya, Max Blade?" Johnny P said from the back.

I went to respond when a car pulled up behind us out of nowhere. Wheels spinning and gaining on us something fierce. Which only meant one thing.

Sure enough, the reds and blues started whirlin' away.

Glancing in my rearview mirror, I mumbled, "Not good, Max Blade..."

The fellas looked behind and shook their heads.

"Not good is right," Gideon said.

Johnny P chuckled and turned back around. "Looks like

one of the Junction's finest might be spoilin' the night before
it lifted off the ground."

"Was I speedin'?" I asked, gripping the wheel harder
and glancing back again, givin' the Breeze some love and
pulling away even as my backside was lit up like a
Christmas tree.

"I'd imagine so," Gideon said, "but...err, shouldn't you
be slowing down?"

"Yeah, Max, about time to give her up and pull over
with the way that county mounty is riding your tail."

I looked back again, keeping on going and figuring out
my options.

Then Junction's finest threw up a siren, jolting everyone
into action.

"Alright, party's over, Max," Gideon said.

"Yeah, partner, pull her over and get this over with,"
Johnny P complained.

Gideon braced himself, the poor guy glistening with
sweat now and his perfectly coiffed hair wilting under the
pressure. "Isn't there something in the Good Book about
rendering unto Caesar what is Caesars?"

"Yeah, Jesus Christ himself said something to that
effect."

I grinned. "But only if you get caught." Then I let out a
yelping *Yee-haw* and floored it. The fellas joined in with
their own duet, but not to the same triumphant tune.

Decisions, decisions. What to do, what to do...

The county mounty, as JP said, which I quite liked.
Had a nice mocking ring to it, which I liked not because I
didn't have a healthy respect for law enforcement, for Mill
Creek's finest, even. Especially since they kept a hefty bar
tab rolling each week.

Naw, I liked it because this particular county mounty

was crimping my style. The night was supposed to be a boys night out. Hadn't had one of those in ages. Since before the pandemic, probably, what with the lockdown and then business snapping back faster than a drunk to a keg from an AA meeting.

Alright, bad analogy. But it was true. I was spent. And tonight was supposed to recharge the batteries.

And this county mounty was freakin' crimpin' my style!

So I did what anyone would do under the circumstances. We still had quite the distance between us, a whole lot of fog, and an open road I knew like the back of my hand.

"I say we outrun him," I said, glancing back in my rearview mirror again, plotting and scheming as those blues and reds kept whirlin' away, the *hee-haw* of the Jack's siren pluckin' my ever livin' nerves.

"Max, are you high?" JP said from the back.

"I can't be part of this," Gideon said.

"Oh, come on. Grow a pair!" I said. "Where's your sense of adventure!"

"You know he knows that it's you!"

"Not with that fog and plume of dirt spinnin' out back. Besides, I've been livin' in these fields all my life. I know when to—"

I slammed on the brakes, cranking the wheel just before one of those neato dirt roads that run between the property line of the farms anchoring the east side of the Junction.

And sending the windbag copper dancing the jitterbug behind to keep from slammin' into my backside.

The fellas went *"Ahh!!"*

I went *"Whee!!"* as I cranked the wheel and then gunned it down the gullet of the road I'd used to race my brother down on Schwinn bikes better equipped for the mechanics of off-road racing than my Breeze.

Which started bobbin' and weavin' and sendin' a whole lot of hurt through our back sides.

I slowed down the Golden Nugget but kept at it, braking again and yankin' the wheel to the right, asking the Universe for a special helping of love to get me out of the jam and carry us safely to destiny. Which, coincidentally, another word I dug, wasn't too far away now.

Of course, the fellas were cussin' me out the whole way, hollerin' at me to stop and turn myself in. Didn't know who was worse, the shyster lawyer or the priest-turned-PI. Either way, the minutes ticked by, counted off by the breeze whisperin' at me through my open-windowed Breeze and soon we were through the fog and coming to a T intersection.

I brought the Golden Nugget to a halt and threw her into *Park*.

"Are you insane?!?" Gideon bellowed, punching me in the shoulder.

"Yeah, pal, I ain't interested in getting slapped with no accessory to evading the po-po charge," JP said from the back, giving me my own slap to the back of my head.

"Would you just listen a second?" I bellowed back, turning off the car underneath a clear sky and full moon, heads of lettuce in neat rows on both sides keeping us company as a symphony of crickets and tree frogs and the Universe-knows-what serenaded us while waiting for the results of my ballsy, but—yes, I'll admit it—foolhardy plot to evade the Junction's finest spit back our results.

A gentle breeze blew through, yes, the Breeze as we waited for the results and caught our breaths, a few of us— ehh-hem, Gideon—near Nervous Nellys as we waited.

Vegetation and cow manure and hay wafted inside as the night continued its symphony outside.

Soon, it was apparent what was what.

I chuckled, then broke into a laugh riding high on the adrenaline bottled up since stopping.

I banged against the steering wheel and let out another "*Yee-haw!!!*" as the truth of it became evident to all.

We'd outran the law, and we won!

And we lived to tell about it!

"Gotta hand it to ya, kiddo," Johnny P said, "you pulled it off."

"And with style," I replied, pulling out onto another road runnin' perpendicular of packed dirt, covered with that weird fog shimmering under the moonlight and chuck full of possibility.

"I think I'm going to be sick," Gideon moaned, the man propping his elbow up on the window and leaning his head against his palm.

Thought it was a bit dramatic. Not like we robbed a bank or nothin'. Just failed to stop for some lame-ass traffic stop.

"Oh, stop it, ya big baby. Crack open that there box of Pabst would ya—"

"No siree!" Johnny P protested, kicking the box away for good measure. "Not with the po-po on our tail like that. I'm not getting wrapped up in some suspicion of being under the influence in a moving vehicle."

I turned around toward the lug. "Whatever! You ain't getting wrapped up in any suspicion of being under nothin'! Besides, I'm driving and if—"

The Golden Nugget suddenly shuddered, the right wheels ramping up something and getting a bit jiggy with it.

"*Keep your eyes on the road!*" the pair bellowed.

I did, righting the ship after off-roading it a bit and getting a bit too close for comfort next to a drainage ditch edging the road. That was a close one, but just another...

"There!"

Gideon leaned forward. "Where there?"

I turned off onto another side road I'd remembered from summers past. Was grown over with grass and yea-high weeds, but no matter. A tripled-wire fence with barbs ran along the north end, one of it collapsed from a downed wood post that I had taken the liberty of pulling from the ground on my lunch break.

Opening the door, I slid out a leg and flashed him my pearly whites. "You'll see."

Without waiting for an answer, I slipped outside into the dead of night, the moon bright, the air cooled and damp and still smelling of static from the front that had pushed through earlier, on top of the vegetation and manure and hay from earlier.

And then I spotted her. Standing up yonder next to a massive oak crowning a grassy hill dead center of the pasture.

I grinned; couldn't help it. It was gonna be a fabulous night.

"You got a case of PBR at the ready, Johnny P?" I yelled behind, keeping my object of affection in view.

"Sure do," he said with not enough enthusiasm for my liking, but whatever. He slammed his door; Gideon followed suit.

I turned around and took the case from the fella, opening up one end and taking out a can. It opened with a soft *crack*, a head of white foam rising but resting just at the lip, the golden pilsner watered down by some Milwaukee, Wisconsin, aquifer or city water source glistening in the moonlight and looking mighty fine after a long day of work—heck, a long *year* with all the corona-crazy!

Handing the case back to JP and gesturing for the fellas to have at it, I threw back the can and took a long swig. Cheap thing, but it was right for the night.

They joined the party, the thrill of the chase and adren-aline-high from fighting the law and winning wearing off now and giving way to a relaxing night out on the country-side, just the fellas and no care in the world.

Gideon climbed the hood to the Golden Nugget and cracked his own can of PBR, *ahh*ing. Johnny P smacked his lips after his first sip, leaning against his car door.

I smiled and looked at the full moon shining down with favor, then held up my can and offered a toast: "*La Hy-em.*"

Johnny P cracked a smile, then stifled a giggle.

I took a swig and swallowed. "What's so funny?"

"It's not La Hy-em. *L'Chaim,*" Gideon said with the scrape of his throat.

I frowned. "Whatever, Mr. Harvard Law—"

"Georgetown Law," he mumbled under his breath before taking a swig, as if embarrassed.

"Whatever again, Mr. Fancy Pants. Just drink your damn beer—"

"The beer I bought with my hard-earned money, you mean?" Johnny P said.

"Technically, I believe it was Gideon's hard-earned money that he then pawned off on you to get his client off on some charge his sweet thing leveled against a client of his

"Whoa, whoa, whoa!" Gideon protested. "Please don't even tell me you're talking about Annabelle Kirkland right now."

I shrugged and took another swig. "Just sayin'. Your

little mamacita seems to be keepin' you in mighty fine business."

"I keep me in mighty fine business, thank you very much."

"Yeah, me too, pal," Johnny P insisted.

I chuckled. "Whatever."

"But Max is right, though," Gideon said, raising his half-drained can. "To life."

"In small-town, Mill-Creek-Junction America," agreed Johnny P, raising his own can.

"With a Pabst Blue Ribbon."

"God bless the U S of A," I echoed, slurping back the rest of Milwaukee's finest and tossing the can to the dirt road with a clunk.

A few seconds later, and a few swigs later, the fellas added to what I assumed was going to be a growing pile by the end of the night.

The three of us cracked open another trio of cans, the nighttime fauna serenading us while we drank in silence. A commodity in short supply in all three of our lives, I'd imagine.

"So, business back to usual, Max?" Gideon asked, slurping back his can.

I did the same then scoffed. "Hardly. Yeah, I mean the patrons have returned, and we're running mighty high tabs all day and all night. But between the continued ordinances and masks and cleaning regime, it's definitely a new normal as they say."

Johnny P grunted, throwing back another swig, then another before draining his second and tossing it to the growing pile. "New normal my..." he opened another can with a crack and went at it again.

Gideon drained his own can and grabbed another PBR,

voicing his own agreement in the silliness of how the country had treated the corona. At this rate, we'd be lucky to last an hour on the two twelve packs we'd brought!

I drained my own and cracked open my third Pabst, the low alcohol starting to work its magic on the third try. "I don't know," I said. "Seems like Covid was a pretty big deal. Still is. More infectious than we thought—"

"But with far fewer deaths than we could have imagined," Johnny P interjected.

I scoffed again, throwing back a swig. "If you call over eight-hundo-thousand far fewer deaths than we could have imagined!"

"Most of which were from nursing homes," Gideon added, "thanks to the failed policies of those knuckle-headed blue-state governors. Basically blew through the driftwood before setting their states on fire!"

"Hey, don't be calling my grandma driftwood, pal!"

Gideon held up an apologetic hand. "Just saying that the reason why we had so many deaths is because of some bright ideas to stuff the nursing homes full of Covid-positive patients, setting off the forest fire of our ongoing nightmare with the most vulnerable of our society."

I drained my can and waved a dismissive hand, tossing the empty can to the growing pile with a rustly clank. "Whatever, Mack. Not interested in getting into a political discussion out in the middle of Farmer Jedediah's cow pasture..."

Johnny P tossed a can to the pile himself. Apparently I had some competition. "Then what are you interested in, Max? Why are we here?"

I threw up a giggle and rubbed my hands together. "Two words."

I paused, standing before the fellas who held their cans

as if holding their breath. Then finished my reveal: "Cow tipping."

"Cow tipping?" Gideon said, looking at me askance.

And yes, he was. Askance, I tell you. His face exuding doubt and disapproval and general mistrust.

Not that I blamed him. The thing was an urban legend through and through.

But Gideon didn't know that.

"Yeah, cow tipping," I said. Sneaking up on an unsuspecting or sleeping upright cow and pushing it over for entertainment."

"Isn't that illegal?"

I scoffed. "Legal, shmegal. It's fun!

"It's also a bit stereotypical," added Johnny P from the peanut gallery.

I twisted up my face with confusion. "Stereotypical?"

"Yeah, the implication that rural citizen types run after such entertainment as cow tipping because of either some lack of alternative living out in the boondocks or because of ignorance of how cows work is stereotypical of the bucktoothed, country bumpkin who don't know any better."

"Hey, I'm a rural citizen type living out in the boondocks!"

Johnny P raised a brow and folded his arms. "My point exactly."

"Whatever."

I slid next to Gideon and put my arm around him, pointing toward the tree perched up on the grassy knoll and the bovine beaut resting on all fours next to it, silhouetted by the light of the full moon it was storybook perfect.

"See that there cow resting up yonder."

"Yeah," he said, following the trajectory of my arm.

"Now, just creep up behind the Betsy, Gideon, and give her a good fright."

"Max..." Johnny P started before I shooed him away and turned toward him with a finger at my lips. Apparently, the man knew as much about the urban legend as I did. And I communicated all I needed to communicate: Shut yer pie hole, pal!

He did, throwing back some more PBR from a can he'd just opened and swiping his grinning mouth with the back of his hand before walking away.

"Alright," Gideon said, voice exuding determination and confidence. "Hold my beer..."

"Whatever you say, partner," I said, grabbing his beer and offering a sideways glance to Johnny P who had his head buried in his chest, arms folded trying not to laugh.

Took everything within me as well not to bust a gut as the man stumbled into the dead of night, determined to tip a cow on Farmer Jed's hilltop.

Johnny P came up to my side as I stood sipping from my PBR, the moon bright and skies clear and the world full of a whole host of possibilities that could end in several different ways for our dear friend Gideon O'Donnell. Nothing dangerous, mind you. Or, well, too dangerous. But a whole lot of ways that would offer a right good show for the night.

Which is what I needed after the hell of a year I'd had.

"He has no idea what's coming, does he?" JP said lowly, arms still crossed and PBR can raised to his mouth as if he were hidden behind the thing in anticipation of what might unfold before his eyes.

Gideon continued onward, leaning to one side and stumbling every few steps after four or five cans of Milwaukee's finest.

"Nope." I took a swig. "Not a clue."

Had to have been not more than two or three minutes and Gideon reached the bovine beaut. He was hunched now and looked like he was turning back toward us for confirmation.

I raised my can of PBR, then raised a fist and pumped it in the air in triumph and victory, encouraging and egging the man on to seal the deal.

Which he did, creeping up behind the Betsy before Johnny P and me heard the echo of a faint *"BOOO!"* from up yonder.

We snickered and laughed and cheered the man who stood statue still as the thing he thought would happen didn't happen.

Instead of falling over from the frightened *boo* of a drunk Junction defense attorney, the bovine beaut seemed to jump from one patch of grass to another, throwing up a moan that shook the fillings in my teeth.

A beat later, they actually did. Not from the protesting cow, but from the rumble of a stampede of Betsy's friends!

Didn't see that one coming.

And neither did Johnny P, judging by the look on his face and the words coming from the former priest that'd make a nun blush from here to Sunday.

Cresting the hill past the tree was a herd of cattle coming to the bovine beaut's rescue! With Gideon running frantically back toward us, stumblin' and bobbin' and weavin' and throwin' up his hand something fierce along with a cry to get our backsides in gear before he had our PBR-drunk hides.

Didn't have to tell me twice.

I darted back to my car, JP hot on my heels. Sliding inside and slamming the door, I roared the Golden Nugget to life, rolling down my window as JP tucked himself in the back and shouted for Gideon to hightail it as the stampede neared.

He replied with a string of not very nice words, but soon he was falling over the hood toward the front passenger's side as the herd pulled up to the fence with the downed post and milled about, as if giving thought to their next steps, plotting their next moves.

I didn't wait for their second act, flooring it and spinning the tires until they caught with purchase on the dirt road and spit us out toward safer ground.

That's when we heard the blast of a shotgun.

Boom-boom-boom went the night, buckshots going this way and that. Probably high in the sky, but still. Had not a clue where or from whom.

Until a mangy voice, all strained and nasally and dead-serious, bellowed, "Git the Sam Hill off my proper if you know what's good fer ya, you lily livered chicken hearted lickspittles!"

Farmer Jedediah himself. The proprietor of the lands where that herd of Betsys and their mates roamed.

Didn't have to tell me twice.

Easing the Golden Nugget back to the main drag and shifting into *Drive*, I floored her toward destiny. Which was anywhere but there!

"Ooh-wee, was that hot as a stack of flapjacks or what?!" I bellowed, smacking the steering wheel on a rush of adrenaline.

Right before Gideon smacked me hard in the arm.

"Oww! What'd you do that—"

"Did you know that was going to happen?" he yelled.

"Did I know what was going to happen?"

"Don't play dumb with me, Maximilian Blade—the *third*!!"

Uhh-ohh...

I rolled down the window, the fog having lifted now but the night breeze and soft scent of the edge of the Junction bringing me down a notch to handle Gideon.

I said, "Might have thought a thing or two might transpire."

"Why you..."

The man went to slug me again when Johnny P intervened, swatting him back and putting him in his place.

"You got played, Gideon, so what?" Johnny P said.

Gideon spun back toward the man. "You were in on this?"

"No, I wasn't in on it! Knew the whole thing was a crock of crap, but didn't expect no herd of wild cattle to come chasing us down." He snickered and then busted into a laugh, settling back in the seat and carrying on.

Which got me going as we continued getting out of Dodge back to Mill Creek before the Universe decided to throw anything else at us. Even caught a smile on Gideon, the man having settled in his seat and accepted he'd been had.

"Well played, Max," he offered. "Well played."

I didn't say anything in return, just grinned and drove on. What a night.

It was a slow drive back, not wanting to test the rest of the Universe's goodwill after the ball of crazy we'd just experienced. But eventually I wound the Golden Nugget through the Junction's countryside and sidled up to the curb outside Max's Place, the brakes offering up a squeaking protest.

Yeah, right back atcha. After what we'd just been through, not in the mood.

Gideon was out first, then Johnny P as I threw the

Breeze into *Park* for another night and shut 'er off, whispering for her to keep our little secrets from a night that was more than I could have bargained for.

"Have to say, you know how to show a couple of fellas a good time, Max," Gideon said as I climbed out into the land of the sleeping. He followed, opening his door and climbing out himself.

Johnny P grunted. "Yeah, never experienced that thing before."

"Which thing?"

I chuckled. "Yeah, evading the po-po or getting chased by a herd of cattle and then shot at by Farmer Jed?"

"All of the above," the fellas said in unison. Which turned into all three of us offering up a hearty laugh that turned into us doubling over with uncontrolled giggles and guffaws, Gideon throwing himself against the hood of the Breeze and Johnny P bending to one knee to control himself while yours truly just let it all hang out with laughter on the side of Main Street.

Felt like eons since I'd laughed. Probably since it had been eons since I'd gotten out and about with those who meant the most to me.

These fellas. Gideon and Johnny P.

These were my brothers, my boys, my friends. And I was better because of them.

STORY 5

HAPPY FRIENDS GIVING

THE DAY WAS GOING to be perfect. The drive from the store back home portended it.

Flat, barren fields frozen solid were covered with a coating of snow under a wide, cheerful sky that made me wish I had my hunting rifle. Just as I saw a pack of does and a few bucks scrounging around for food as I barreled through the main county road back to Mill Creek Junction with a trunkful of last-minute pickups from the grocery store. Made it out of Meyer's General alive, just barely, and now was pushing sixty through our rural slice of small-town America in the heart of the Midwest, a thin layer of unplowed packed snow crunching under my BMW's winter snow tires.

Was heading home with the rest of the goods needed for the day's festivities after my buddy Max Blade sent me on a wild goose chase through the store for the final touchings on his Thanksgiving dinner masterpiece. Which was a bit ironic, because I was hosting said Thanksgiving dinner masterpiece at my house. No matter. Just glad I made it out alive!

Place closed at noon, and there was old man Fred Meyer, working the registers and working the crowd of last-minute holiday shoppers fetching this and that ingredient for the perfect au gratin potatoes or sweet potato hash or raspberry cobbler recipe. Barely got in and out of the joint myself, and was surprised the store was still opened to begin with. Saw two guys nearly go to blows after one of them took the last of Meyer's turkeys. Thankfully, some stock boy found another dozen, but visions of representing one of them in court were flashing through my head, wondering which one would have the stronger case. Why the heck people waited until the last minute to get what they need for Thanksgiving Day was beyond me. Although, I suppose I was the chump who was standing in line with a cartful of Thanksgiving necessities, so what do I know!

My phone buzzed with an incoming text. It was Max Blade.

'Gideon, my man. Where're the goods?'

I rolled my eyes at the man's impatience, texting back simply: *'On the way.'*

A few beats later: *'Well hop to it, O'Donnell. Don't want to disappoint your chickadee ;)'*

I scoffed and tossed the phone on the passenger's seat, shaking my head.

I assumed Max was referring to Annabelle Kirkland, the Junction assistant prosecuting attorney who was slated to join me and Max and a few others for a mid-afternoon dinner at my place. We'd gone out a few times for drinks and general chit-chat, but I wouldn't categorize it as anything but platonic friendship at this point. She certainly wasn't my chickadee! Max better behave tonight, that's all I have to say.

I rolled down my driver's side window and cranked the

heat, something I did once a year on Thanksgiving to remind me I was still alive. The crisp air laced with burning wood from fireplaces a few miles away and dead leaves in clumpy piles along the road slapped me in the face, amplified by my BMW's hot ventilation.

Just the way I liked it. My own taste of heaven.

Bruce Springsteen was belting "Born in the USA" which seemed appropriate, given the holiday, the best there was.

Thanksgiving.

Should be Christmas and Easter tying for that title, given my upbringing in the Church and all. And it wasn't that I didn't appreciate them, but there was something about setting aside a day to remember our blessings with family and friends that just did something in me the others didn't. Probably helped I was stuck in small-town USA, which not only made you grateful for what you had, but also was the perfect setting to commemorate America's holiday.

And let me tell you, the spirit of Norman Rockwell was alive and well in Mill Creek Junction on Thanksgiving Day.

Or so we hoped, the whole lot of us turning into pseudo-mediums channelling his spirit and trying our darndest to recreate his famous *Freedom from Want* painting in our own neck of the U.S. of A. woods.

The tables in our turn-of-the century craftsman homes were decked out to the nines with bleached-white table clothes and fancy bone china in dining rooms with the same viney wallpaper, windows all laced up. The good silverware, the kind actually made from silver, were dragged up from musty basements or down from dusty attics and set like chess pieces waiting to make their moves.

Kitchens were near a boiling point from all-morning cooking frenzies and from frayed-nerve tempers over battles about what to cook and how to cook and when to cook this-that-and-the-other—or from heated discussion about politics and sports and *Dancing with the Stars* that had no place in either the kitchen or at Thanksgiving, as far as I was concerned.

Yep, that was Thanksgiving in the Junction alright. All aspiring for the Norman Rockwell recreation while usually ending up with something more along the lines of Clark Griswold.

As for me and my household, I liked to keep things as simple and stress-free as possible. Helped Mom and Dad were visiting my grandparents on the East Coast, Gramps and Grammy still kicking it at ninety-two in a nursing home but needing some company. Which was fine, because sometimes after a holiday get together at the O'Donnell household, one needed a separate holiday just to recuperate!

Growing up, Thanksgiving at Mom's and Dad's was less *Leave it to Beaver* and more *Home Improvement.* More that Clark Griswold I was talking about and less Norman Rockwell. Dad was the one who generally did all the cooking, and the guy would try out something new and fancy in the kitchen, or had some mishap stringing up the Christmas lights, or got ornery after the Lions biffed it in the fourth quarter, as always—only to end in a disaster that wound either him or me or both of us at Urgent Care. It was a good time with good family memories celebrating our blessings, just usually more than we bargained for.

Speaking of which, I should probably phone in and wish them a happy Thanksgiving.

It was just past noon now, the sun tilted and riding lower as I turned onto Main Street, the barren trees sending strange shadows across the road up ahead. I told Siri to call my mother, and the phone complied.

A few seconds later, Mama was heard saying, "Hey, baby! Happy Thanksgiving!" in her perfect Baltimorese.

"Happy Thanksgiving, Mama. Dad there with you?"

There was a crackling and then a thud on the other line. Sounded like I'd lost her.

"Mama?"

More static and muffled voices.

"Mama?"

"Hey, son."

It was Dad. "Hey, yourself, Pops. Happy Thanksgiving. How are you and Mama faring out east?"

"Well, Mama's fixin' to wring both your Gramps and Grammy's necks before the afternoon's out, that's how."

I chuckled. "Sounds about right."

More static and another round of thuds before Mama was heard asking for the phone back.

"You there, baby?" she said.

"Sounds like you're having a blast back east."

"Ba! That's one way of putting it. How 'bout you. J'eat yet?"

I smiled. There was that slice of Mid-Atlantic American English I knew well.

"No, we haven't eaten yet. Coming home now with some last minute things from Fred Meyer's joint."

"What? You went shoppin' on Turkey Day?"

I scoffed. "Believe me, I know. A glutton for punishment. You can thank Max Blade for that."

"*Psht.* He's always draggin' ya into trouble."

"It wasn't like that. Not this time at least. Remember, I'm having some of my friends over—"

"That's right. The singleton's Turkey Day festivity."

"Yes, Mama. Us five are singles. And I prefer to call our festivity a Friends Giving."

"If'n you say so."

"Anyway, doesn't matter. How are Gramps and Grammy? Send them my love, will you?"

Mama sighed. "Not good, hon."

I sat up straight, furrowing my brow with worry. "What do you mean, not good?"

"As in d'mencha, not good."

I eased in a steadying breath at the word. Dementia. No, not Gramps and Grammy.

My mother continued, "Mama thinks tomorrow is the Selma march. And your daddy near well had to strap Gramps to the chair to keep him from up and driving both of them down to that damn bridge!"

"Selma march?" I asked, not following.

"Yeah, you remember the stories grammy told from back in their days in the Deep South, bussing down to Alabama from Baltimore that March of '65 to join the protests against Jim Crow laws."

I did. How the police hosed down Gramps and Grammy crossing the bridge, then let loose the German shepherds that had maimed Grammy's right cheek and tore off Gramps's left thumb. Being adopted into a black family off the stoop of a Junction fire station, with skin whiter than Lake Michigan sand, meant I'd confronted America's original sin of slavery, the buying and selling of black bodies for profit and the ongoing injustices of keeping those bodies underfoot, far faster than any of my white peers.

Couldn't not confront it with the stories I heard from Gramps and Grammy.

And now to hear they were slipping into dementia, to know their stories and experiences would fade away from memory into the ether of broken neural synapses made me sad.

And also thankful—*grateful* I'd been adopted into that heritage and given the O'Donnell name that had survived generations from the original slave-owning Irish merchant from Baltimore, Maryland. Made me who I was. Gave me the vision for my life and all I fought for with my law practice, fighting for—

A loud thud followed by a *thrump-thrump-thrump-thrump-thrump* was heard under my car.

Passenger's side, rear.

"What the heck..."

Nearly dropped the phone at the sound that was luckily more muffled and thwapping than clangy and clattery.

At least I hoped I was on the lucky end of this BMW bargain.

The noise kept at it, the *thrump-thrump-thrump-thrump-thrump* strumming a mean beat that meant nothing good.

"Uh, Mama, I need to go."

"Everything alright, baby?"

"Not sure. Something doesn't sound right with my car. I should go."

Was nearly home now, about half a mile. What they say about accidents probably rings true of car troubles, too. And on Thanksgiving of all days!

"Hope it's not serious, baby. You think you should call an am'blance?"

I smiled. There was that Baltimorese shining through again.

"I'll be fine, Mama. It's the BMW. Just making some racket."

It was getting louder now, and the car was vibrating, the rear end dragging something fierce.

"*Psht.* That's German engineering for ya," Mama complained. "Shoulda gone with a Ford, like your daddy advised. Found on road dependable, that's what Gramps always said."

"Yes, ma'am." Though I'd always heard it as *Found on road dead.*

"You be safe now, ya hear?"

"Yes, ma'am. I'll text when I find out."

We said our goodbyes and love, offering another round of 'Happy Thanksgiving' to Daddy and my grandparents, then hung up the phone.

Far down Main Street off from the state highway and approaching Mill Creek's downtown, I pulled the bimmer to the curb and put her in 'Park'—behind a 90s Ford Escort, of all things.

I shut her off and stepped out into the crisp November early afternoon, the sun still high and tilted and taking the bite out of the bitter wind blowing off from Lake Michigan three counties away. As it should be on Thanksgiving Day.

I inched around toward the right rear. And there it was.

Flat tire.

On Thanksgiving Day!

"Just my luck..."

I crouched down next to it, spending the next few minutes making my assessments and coming up with nothing but the obvious. A flat tire.

Wasn't about to change the dang thing, not when I had a turkey in the oven and a Max Blade playing Wolfgang Puck in my kitchen.

Not only did I spend a stress-filled hour at the grocery store scrounging around for the last bits to my Thanksgiving soiree, I got news Gramps's and Grammy's minds were heading downhill fast on top of getting a flat tire.

Not the way I wanted the day to go. Not in the slightest.

But no use whining about it. Especially on Thanksgiving. And especially on *this* Thanksgiving with all the crazy we've survived this year!

I popped the trunk and grabbed the three bags, man-handling two in one arm and one in the other. Then I set off down Main Street toward home several blocks away.

The sun was behind me and angled all wrong for the jaunt through the Junction, the rays obscured by large trees waving their naked arms around in the bluster, buildings casting long shadows now across the sidewalk and street as it dipped toward mid-afternoon. Although, the more I trudge across town in my down North Face jacket, the more I appreciated the shadows creeping into Mill Creek.

The walk was pretty quiet, the occasional couple strolling and nodding a greeting, kiddos racing down the wide-open Main Street that had been cleared of the earlier snow. Leaves that had lost their color weeks ago blew in scattered bunches across the sidewalk. Darkened storefronts greeted me at each block, makeshift "Closed for the Holiday Weekend" signs taped haphazardly across doors and windows. The way it should be, really, on Thanksgiving Day. Especially after the crazy year the Universe threw at us—the Junction and all America, the world.

Nothing a stuffed turkey with all the fixings couldn't fix, friends and family gathered with a few bottles of wine to soothe the soul, along with thickly sliced turkey, ample helpings of green bean casserole, and a dollop of cranberry sauce.

If ever there was a time to give thanks for the blessings

of this life—for the blessing of *life*—especially to the Lord Almighty for seeing us through, this was the year!

A few turns toward Mill Creek Junction's residential side of town and several more blocks, I finally reached home. Woodsmoke from hearths across the neighborhood hovered over the street along with the smells of Thanksgiving meals wafting out of open windows. Cars were beginning to fill up driveways now and spill out along the street—giving my spirit the festive juice it needed after hauling the pickups home.

The garage door was still opened from when I left for Meyer's General. Felt like hours ago, and my nose and fingers were now starting to tingle from the November chill. I beelined it for the side entrance into the house. Jostling two bags in one arm and holding the other one with the other stiffly against the door, I reached for the handle, my fingers grasping for purchase but finding no leads. I contorted myself into a pretzel trying to keep the goods from crashing to the floor while at the same time trying to get inside my house.

"Max Blade..." I mumbled as I continued fishing for the handle. "Just had to send me out on Thanksgiving morning."

Which was ironic because Max's joint back in town off Main Street, with all the things he cooked up at his bar and grill, probably rivaled the backroom of Fred's joint, with all his stock in meat and vegetables and other foodstuff. I was still a little hot under the collar that the guy had forgotten a laundry list of items and sent me to go fetch.

Hence the late morning run to Meyer's General just after he had arrived to get his cooking on before our guests arrived. Resulting in the flat tire and now my undershirt soaking wet from perspiration.

If you ask me, the guy was just cheaping out, but whatever. I was happy to get the rest of the fixings, given I was hosting the afternoon dinner. Tried to plan the whole thing from the get-go, but Max insisted on making it all from scratch himself. Asked why he didn't just host us at his joint in the first place, but he liked the way my KitchenAid range cooked things compared to the GE electric stove in his upstairs apartment and his industrial-strength sets of burners in the bar's kitchen.

Whatever, and why ever, there I was. The rest of the goods sandwiched against my house's garage side door leading into my two-story craftsman I hoped to God was still intact!

"Max Blade..." I groaned, still fishing for the knob, "I'm gonna kill you."

The door suddenly opened, turning my equilibrium totally against me so that—

"Thought I heard ya yappin'—"

—toppled inside right past the door.

Max cried out with a start. Then I responded with a muffled yelp of my own through the brown grocery bag.

The next few seconds were like something out of the Matrix, the two of us crashing into one another and trying to save the bags of groceries before they crashed to the floor while we both tried to save ourselves from breaking a bone.

Somehow, we managed to accomplish both goals. Max swiped both bags from my one arm while managing to plant both feet on the wood floors and stay upright. I slid to my knees and bear-hugged the other bag.

"Nice moves, partner!" Max said, handling the two bags in one arm and offering his other hand.

I took it, a bit winded from the whirlwind last-minute

shopping and the near-death experience getting back into my home.

"Thanks. That's what four years of high school football will do for you."

"That's right. The good ol' Mill Creek Junction Trojans." The guy snickered like a high schooler. Trojans wasn't the best of names, especially during the '90s when the government type were trying to stamp down the blooming epidemic of teen pregnancies.

I threw him a frown that let him know I wasn't in the mood, then stood armed with my one bag and inhaled a satisfying breath, the baking bird and roasting vegetables and baking bread competing for attention.

"Wow, that smells amazing, Max!" I said, slapping the guy on the shoulder and feeling more relaxed now that I was home after all the crazy stressful shopping and knowing that we had all we needed for the day that was quickly fading. Which meant it was T-minus one hour until the guests arrived!

Man, hosting was for the birds...

Max grinned. "Don'tcha know it, partner! Wait till you see what I got cooking. Literally."

He brushed past me through my living room, a large picture window overlooking my neighborhood fogged over from all the cooking going on in the next room.

Reminded me of Thanksgiving from ages past, when both Daddy and Mama spent all morning and early afternoon toiling away in a kitchen that was more like a closet. There was the turkey, of course, baking away in the oven under mounds of butter, so there was that added browned butter that accompanied the sharp scent of baking bird. Add to that the sweet aromas of corn and beans; collard greens fried in a pan of oil and bacon, Mama's specialty;

baking bread and a sweet apple pie. The Junction had nothing on Turkey day, as Mama called it, at the O'Donnell's!

Though, Max was coming close.

After slumping his groceries on my granite island, he started roaming the kitchen, from cooking thing to cooking thing. A dirty, faded white apron was tied loosely around his neck and waist, clipboard and pencil in hand.

I set my bag next to the other two and planted my hands on my hips, taking in the view.

It was more organized than I would have taken Max for, the wrappers and boxes and leftovers of this vegetable and that vegetable seemingly put away in the trash. A glass lid rapped a *pitter-patter* beat on a pot resting on my range, boiling yams or sweet potatoes. Never could understand the difference between the two. A mound of aluminum foil was seen through the little window looking into the oven. The bird. A tray of rolls sat dutifully on the counter under a towel, and a cherry pie was waiting to join the bird inside the oven.

But wait...

I leaned over a pan of green balls cut in half and resting in a large concave pan on the main burner, waiting to fry in a sheen of green oil, the strong scent of garlic and black pepper and something else I couldn't quite place rising from the middle.

"What are these?" I asked, twisting up my face at the sight of something I'd never seen at any Thanksgiving dinner this side of the Grand River.

"Brussels sprouts," Max said.

I turned to him. "Wait, what?"

He furrowed his brow, pencil hovering above the clipboard. "Like I said...Brussels sprouts."

"Who cooks brussel sprouts for Thanksgiving?"

He put the pencil behind his ear and folded his arms, clipboard banging the side of his apron. "First, it's Brussels*ssss* sprouts. With an *s*. Like the country."

"Yeah, yeah. Whatever. And it's a city. The capital of Belgium."

"Second..." he went on, ignoring me, "civilized people cook brussel sprouts for Thanksgiving."

"Don't you mean Brussels*ssss* sprouts with an *s*?"

Max huffed and withdrew his pencil, then dipped his head and got back to—whatever it was he was doing.

A clock chimed once from the living room. The grandfather gifted to me by Gramps after graduation from law school. I checked my watch and startled.

Thirty minutes until showtime!

"We should check the turkey," I insisted, shuffling over to the oven.

"Probably a good idea," Max said, setting the clipboard down on the island with a clatter. "Wouldn't want the star attraction missing out on the show. No understudy to this here turkey, that's for sure!"

Ignoring the man, I opened the oven and withdrew the deep oval pan holding the mound of foil I'd spotted earlier. It was heavier than I remembered, the thing jostling as I carefully set it on the stove for a look-see.

"That's a mighty big bird..." Max muttered from behind. "You sure you followed the cookin' instructions right?"

"Yeees," I said, slowly nodding my head as I peeled back the foil. "A ten-pound bird, times twenty minutes per pounds, divided by sixty leads to a little over three-and-a-half hours." I folded my arms. "Simple math."

"Then why ain't the popper poppin'?"

"Huh?"

Max pointed over my shoulder at the red knob still stuck down in the white prob stuck inside the turkey.

My stomach slumped toward the tiled floor at the sight. I resisted glancing at my watch, knowing I had put the turkey in just before I left for Meyer's General. Should be about ready.

"I don't know..." was all I managed. "Maybe it's broken."

"Well, do you have a digital thermometer?"

"Uhh..." I pushed off the stove and went to the island, opening a drawer. I started rummaging through the utensils, coming up dry and wishing I had organized my kitchen better.

"You know, a clean kitchen is a healthy kitchen," Max crooned from another drawer.

"It's clean!"

"Well, then a well-organized kitchen is a healthy kitchen!"

We rummaged through my kitchen utensils for several minutes, moving from one drawer to the next and crossing paths, retracing our steps.

"Found one!" Max finally said. He was holding a round disc with a long stem. "Not digital, but it'll do the job."

I took it, one end of my mouth rising. "Mom's old-fashioned cooking thermometer."

Felt a bit of nostalgia holding the long metal stem with a large round dial, memories from Thanksgivings past popping like champagne bubbles.

Max snatched it back. "Old-fashioned is right. It'll have to do..."

He went back to the oven and opened the door. Then he peeled back the foil and stuck the device in the bird.

"Now, we wait."

The seconds ticked by as the red arrow made its way around the large round dial. We both instinctively leaned toward the thing, waiting for its final verdict.

Suddenly, the arrow slowed. We had our verdict.

Just a hair above 150.

Max muttered something under his breath as he pulled the thermometer out from the bird, a stream of oily liquid leaking out.

"I don't get it," I said as he wrapped the foil back over the turkey hump. "Should be nearly finished by now!"

"Get the oven door for me, will ya?"

He lifted the large roasting pan by the handles; I got the door.

"When did you put the thing in the oven?" he grunted as he slid the pan back into place.

"Before you showed up and before I headed over to Meyer's General. Timed it to a T."

Closing the door, he put his hands on his hips. "And how big is our undercooked bird?"

"Ten pounds."

Max scoffed, then laughed. "No way that heifer is ten pounds."

"Fowl. It's a turkey!"

"Whatever, where's the *fowl's* packaging."

I pointed to under the sink. "The garbage."

"Garbage?" he exclaimed. "How the hey-ho-day we gonna know how long to cook the very not-ten-pound turkey we got roastin' in that fancy oven of yours?"

I shrugged. "I don't know. Guesstimate?"

He gasped. "Guesstim—" Then he shook his head and made for the trash. "You don't *guesstimate* with cooking. Especially a turkey, for cryin' out loud! Last thing we want is to overcook the thing. Dry turkey on Turkey Day ain't right. Downright sacrilege."

"Yeah, yeah, yeah," I complained over his shoulder as he waded his arms through the trash.

"And you definitely don't wanna undercook the thing. Salmonella ain't what it's cracked up to be."

The man huffed and started flinging the garbage now on the floor. Dirty, soaking paper towel; leftover sweet potato slices, or yams, whichever was which; and now slices of onions and wilting Brussels sprout leaves.

"Whoa, whoa, whoa!" I cried, putting a hand on his shoulder to stop the insanity.

He shrugged me off and kept digging, finally pulling his arm out of the bin. It was wet and slimy and caked with my morning coffee grounds. But he was holding a black mesh bag with a square plastic card attached with a label stuck to it.

The turkey bag.

Squinting, Max brought it up to his face. He frowned and shook his head. "Yeah, you've got yourself a twenty pounder, partner."

"What?" I exclaimed. "Twenty pounds?"

I snatched the label slick with garbage from Max and held it up to my face now. Furrowing my brow, I examined the poundage, the numbers smeared and faded from being submerged in the trash.

He was right. Twenty pounds.

I sighed and tossed the label back into the trash can. "How much longer is this going to set us back?"

He shook his head. "Not long. Just another hour or so."

First the flat, then an undercooked bird? What else could go wrong?

Ding-dong the front door sounded.

I checked my watch, then sighed. The guests had arrived.

Grinning, Max clapped his hands and rubbed them together. "Looks like we got company!" He grabbed a bottle of wine and started working the cork with a bottle opener. "Reset that timer on the oven, will ya? An hour henceforth should do the trick."

An hour henceforth?

"Oh, I'll check the timer," I muttered as I sauntered over to the stove. "And then some..."

Crouching, I set the digital timer for an hour and then turned up the heat on our bird. Just a smidge. He deserved it.

Max made for the front bearing two glasses of wine. I pushed passed him into the living room, taking one of the glasses on the way to the front door.

"I'm hosting, remember?" I said, hustling past before he could protest.

"Only because you own the joint. I'm the one that's been slavin' away!"

"While I was negotiating all the crazy at Meyer's General because you didn't bring half your ingredients!" I reached the door first and went for the knob. "Still don't know what you used all that stuff for anyhow."

Max grabbed my arm before I could open the door.

"Let's do it together," he said. "Two hosts with the most. Your house, my food. Seems only fair."

"Uh, well—"

"Never hosted Turkey Day before. Never had a place like this to do it in." Max swept the large living room, a sheepish, embarrassed grin playing across his face. "That's not even touchin' on the kinds of SPAM and mac n' cheese meals we had growing up. So I've sorta liked getting into the spirit of it all."

Max's admissions sent a reorienting jolt through my spine that reminded me what this day was all about: friends, family, and food. The moment sure got my head back on straight after a day of frenzied frustration.

I smiled and nodded. "Deal. We're duel hosts."

He smiled and nodded back. "Let's just hope not dueling hosts, for your sake. You know I'd whip your bottom from here to the U.P."

I scoffed. "Whatev—"

The doorbell intercepted my reply. Two impatient *ding-dong-ding-dongs*, then a third to put an exclamation point on it.

"Alright!" the two of us said in unison. Us hosts.

I opened the door, and the two of us greeted our guests.

There stood Annabelle Kirkland and Peter Young. Not together, just standing together, both bundled in dark wool coats and red scarves.

"Happy Thanksgiving!" the pair said in unison.

And popping up behind them was someone I hadn't expected.

Tracy Nolland, editor-in-chief of the *Mill Creek Junction Guardian.*

My face started to fall, a few awkward memories of our on-again-off-again dating surfacing. But I cleared my throat and smiled.

I went to offer a greeting when Max popped over my shoulder and whistled. "Feel like there was a rumor about the two of—"

"Shut it, Max," I hissed through gritted teeth before putting on a false grin. "Tracy, didn't know you were coming."

She matched my grin with a bemused one of her own, drawing me in with her eyes as those long, silky legs under a cream wool coat carried her along on perfectly placed feet up my front sidewalk.

"Me neither," she offered. "But my bestie, Annabelle Kirkland here, said I should come."

"Great!" Max said. "The more the merrier in my book."

I chuckled weakly. "Yeah, that's real great. But I only planned on five."

"Oh, well, my girlfriend isn't able to make it," Peter said.

"There you go, then!" Max offered. "It's like the Universe planned it, or something."

"Exactly." Tracy shoved a still-warm round dish covered in aluminum foil toward me and took the glass of wine I was holding, then winked. "Don't mind if I do."

"Me neither," Annabelle said, swiping Max's own wine glass with a giggle.

"Hey!" Max complained, folding his arms in a huff.

On top of all that had already happened, now my sort-of ex-girlfriend shows up to my Thanksgiving dinner? Couldn't figure what sort of penance this was for, but I must have been a bad boy to deserve this!

"How about we skip past the do-si-doin' at Gideon's threshold," Max complained, "and get back inside. My nose is froze!"

He turned back, and I held out my hand for the three guests, Annabelle, my latest interest, followed by my last, and then Peter.

"Sorry your girlfriend couldn't make it," I said, closing the door behind Peter. "What's her name?"

"Lexi. She wanted to come, she really did. Wanted to meet the gang that's been so great to me the past few months as I've settled into things."

"Ba!" Max cried out from the kitchen. "This is only the honeymoon season, son. Just wait til the new year. We'll put you through the wringer soon enough."

I shook my head. "Ignore him. Sorry Lexi wasn't able to make it. What happened?"

We joined the others around the granite island, setting down our dishes as Max poured two more glasses of red wine, then one for Peter. I took one and nodded my thanks, throwing back a gulp that filled my mouth with black cherry and vanilla and tobacco. I deserved it.

"She wanted to come," Peter went on, "she really did. But she came down with a nasty bug."

Max gasped. "Is it the ro?"

Peter raised a brow and glanced at me. "The ro?"

I said, "He means coronavirus."

"Ahh. I guess that's the assumption nowadays. No, a stomach bug. I'll spare you the details. Enough said."

"We'll have her over soon," I said, uncovering the foil from Tracy's dish. "A pumpkin pie."

"Homemade."

"Didn't know you could cook."

"You didn't ask." She winked at me again before throwing back a gulp of wine herself.

This was going to be a long night.

"Gideon screwed up the turkey," Max said, clipboard back in hand. "So it's gonna be awhile until we're ready to eat."

"I did *not* screw up the turkey!" I shouted in defense.

"I'd say confusing a ten-pound bird with a twenty-pounder screwing up—"

"Boys!" Tracy shouted. "Put the swords away."

"Yeah, it's Thanksgiving, for crying out loud,"

Annabelle joined in. "Talk less, drink more. That's what my meemaw would say."

"Cheers to that," Peter said with raised glass, joining in the interference effort.

We all raised a glass, and then Max busied himself with a few things on the stove and checked on his Brussels sprouts in the oven, adding Annabelle's green bean casserole dish to the mix. House was really smelling heavenly now, the creams and sauces, garlic and spices combining with the bird still cooking away to set the festive Thanksgiving mood.

The four of us went to the living room while Max finished with the clipboard, but not before I opened another bottle of wine and took it with; we were gonna need it!

Soon, Max joined us after all was set in the kitchen. Said we should be good to go soon once the turkey timer went off.

The room filled with conversations about Annabelle's work at the prosecuting office, about the scoop Tracy got on Mayor Goodall's election shenanigans, about Max's renovation plans for the bar, about Peter's first few months as head priest or minister or whatever of the Baptist church downtown. I tried to engage, but my mind was elsewhere.

The turkey.

I checked my watch, concerned about the main event after all that went wrong today. Surprised the timer hadn't gone off yet. But with all that had happened, and the false start with the afternoon and trying to right the turkey ship, I was completely turned around when it came to the time.

One thing was for certain: No way in hot Hades was I going to screw up the turkey!

Not on my li—

"What's that smell?" Tracy complained, snapping me back to the moment.

"Smell?" Max asked.

"Smells like something's burning."

Raising her nose, Annabelle took in a breath. "Not burning, charred."

Tracy nodded. "Definitely overdone."

I gasped; so did Max.

"The turkey!" we said as one.

"Turkey?" Tracy said.

I jumped to my feet and made for the kitchen.

"I thought you set the timer on that damn bird!" Max complained, jumping up next and dashing after me.

"I thought *you* set the timer!" I shouted from behind, skidding across the wood floor and reaching for the oven door. What I saw stopped me cold.

A trace amount of gray, gaseous something rising from the vent at the back of the stovetop.

"Me? It's your dang stove, and it was your dang fault we're in this pickle in the first—" he stopped short, a squeaking gasp replacing his next words. "Is that smoke?"

It was...

I opened the oven, more of the gray, gaseous something pluming out in billowing breaths.

"Egads, man! What's the temp on this thing? Has to be way past three-twenty-five."

"Uh," I stammered, "I may have goosed it a little."

"By how much?"

"To four?"

He turned to me with wide eyes. "Four hundo?" he exclaimed.

"Tried to speed up the process."

"Oh, you sped it up alright!"

"What's the matter, Gideon?" asked Tracy.

I ignored her, instinctively reaching for the roasting pan now.

And scorching myself without thinking!

Thankfully, the back of my brain—the lizard part that had helped my species survive mastodons and saber-tooth tigers, and keep from burning down the forest at the first discovery of fire—that subconscious part stayed my hand completely before I grabbed hold of it wholesale.

I yelped and snapped my arms back.

"Gideon!" Tracy and Annabelle yelled together, reaching toward me. Sort of touched actually, the two women I'd dated rallying emotional support.

Fingers burned like a mother, though, the tips of every one of my digits sans my pinkie bright red and tingling with burn.

"Here, let me..." Max said, pushing past me as I shook off the pain, hands gloved.

He pulled out the mound covered with glittering foil and set it on the granite island. Then he started peeling back the layers of aluminum.

Didn't want to look.

Removing all he needed for the reveal, Max stepped back and folded his arms. It was worse than I'd feared.

"Crispy heifer, ain't it?" he crooned.

"Fowl," I growled, the bird's husk looking like tanned leather glanced by charcoal.

Charred is right.

Now I groaned, leaning against my sink counter and hanging my head in shame.

"Sorry for screwing up Thanksgiving, guys..." I mumbled.

"At least we've got Brussels sprouts," Max said, trying to offer moral support in his own way.

A snorting laugh escaped Tracy. Then Annabelle offered a giggle that rolled into the next, and then some more. Followed by Peter letting out his own snickers. Which led to Max just letting it go.

I glanced up, the ends of my mouth curling upward as the room lost it. Now I did too, the emotion from the day spilling out at the thought I'd not only over cooked our bird, I'd burned it! We had seriously torched the thing. Now all we had was Brussels sprouts to show for the day—of all things!

"Seriously, guys. Sorry I ruined Thanksgiving."

"Oh, stop!" Max said. "You didn't ruin' nothin'."

"I burned our bird, for crying out loud."

Peter put a hand on my shoulder and offered me my glass of wine.

I took it and nodded in thanks, throwing back a mouthful.

"Look, my friend," he said, "Thanksgiving isn't about the food."

"Although a nicely cooked turkey don't hurt none, neither..." Max added.

"Drink your win, Max," Tracy said, shoving his glass back in his hand. He took it and obeyed.

I could see Peter trying to suppress a grin. He went on. "It's about giving thanks for all that the Lord has blessed us with. Friends and family. A roof over our heads. Jobs and good health. It's like what the Jewish poet wrote in Psalm 9: *'I will give thanks to the Lord with my whole heart; I will tell of all your wonderful deeds.'*"

"Leave it up to preacherman to preach," Max said, slapping Peter on his back.

"No, no. Not a sermon. Just a thought."

I smiled. "And a mighty good one at that."

"Don't know about you," Peter went on, "but the Lord's done some mighty wonderful deeds in my life this year."

I stood off from the sink counter with an idea. "Then why don't we share them."

"Share them?" Max asked, brow raised and downing another mouthful of wine.

"Yeah, share what we can give thanks for. We may not have a turkey, but we've got each other, and our stories."

Tracy raised her glass. "I'll drink to that."

"Me too," said Annabelle, raising her own glass. "Well said."

Then we got to it, sharing about the blessing of cases won for justice and stable business despite the economic implosion; of new relationships and new opportunities, and the continued health of old relationships and old opportunities; of the newfound delight in the simple, the ordinary, the mundane, with the kinds of things we take for granted in a year turned upside down—like grocery stores stocked with toilet paper and canned goods, like a night out for dinner and drinks with friends, like face-to-face worship in our faith communities.

We might not have had a turkey, but we sure had our stories, our friendship.

We had each other. A true "friends giving," I suppose.

After all, that's what Thanksgiving is all about.

EXPLORE MORE OF MILL CREEK JUNCTION

Welcome to a new story world inspired by such fictional towns as John Grisham's Clanton, Mississippi, and Stephen King's Castle Rock, Maine.

Get to know this world one character, one setting, one event and situation at a time. You're sure to find some of your own story in theirs, while being entertained and inspired for the journey.

Visit www.millcreekjunction.com for more details about the world and a list of short and long-form fiction, following the lives of real people living life and exploring faith.

GET YOUR FREE THRILLER

Building a relationship with my readers is one of my all-time favorite joys of writing! Once in a while I like to send out a newsletter with giveaways, free stories, pre-release content, updates on new books, and other bits on my stories.

Join my insider's group for updates, giveaways, and your free novel—a full-length action-adventure story in my *Order of Thaddeus* thriller series. Just tell me where to send it.

Follow this link to subscribe:
www.jabouma.com/free

ALSO BY J. A. BOUMA

Nobody should have to read bad religious fiction—whether it's cheesy plots with pat answers or misrepresentations of the Christian faith and the Bible. So J. A. Bouma tells compelling, propulsive stories that thrill as much as inspire, offering a dose of insight along the way.

Order of Thaddeus **Action-Adventure Thriller Series**

Ichthus Chronicles **Sci-Fi Apocalyptic Series**

Apostasy Rising / Season 1, Episode 1

Apostasy Rising / Season 1, Episode 2

Apostasy Rising / Season 1, Episode 3

Apostasy Rising / Season 1, Episode 4

Apostasy Rising / Full Season 1 (Episodes 1 to 4)

Apocalypse Rising / Season 2, Episode 1

Apocalypse Rising / Season 2, Episode 2

Apocalypse Rising / Season 2, Episode 3

Apocalypse Rising / Season 2, Episode 4

Apocalypse Rising / Full Season 2 (Episodes 1 to 4)

Faith Reimagined **Spiritual Coming-of-Age Series**

A Reimagined Faith • Book 1

A Rediscovered Faith • Book 2

Mill Creek Junction **Short Story Series**

The New Normal • Book 1

My Name's Johnny Pope • Book 2

Joy to the Junction! • Book 3

The Ties that Bind Us • Book 4

Get all the latest short stories at: www.millcreekjunction.com

Find all of my latest book releases at: www.jabouma.com

ABOUT THE AUTHOR

J. A. Bouma believes nobody should have to read bad religious fiction—whether it's cheesy plots with pat answers or misrepresentations of the Christian faith and the Bible. So he wants to do something about it by telling compelling, propulsive stories that thrill as much as inspire, while offering a dose of insight along the way.

As a former congressional staffer and pastor, and award-nominated bestselling author of over forty religious fiction and nonfiction books, he blends a love for ideas and adventure, exploration and discovery, thrill and thought. With graduate degrees in Christian thought and the Bible, and armed with a voracious appetite for most mainstream genres, he tells stories you'll read with abandon and recommend with pride—exploring the tension of faith and doubt, spirituality and culture, belief and practice, and the gritty drama that is our collective pilgrim story.

When not putting fingers to keyboard, he loves vintage jazz vinyl, a glass of Malbec, and an epic read—preferably together. He lives in Grand Rapids with his wife, two kiddos, and rambunctious boxer-pug-terrier.

www.jabouma.com • jeremy@jabouma.com

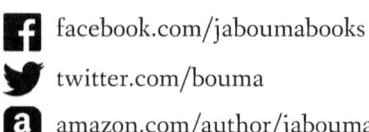

facebook.com/jaboumabooks

twitter.com/bouma

amazon.com/author/jabouma